dragons
WORLDS AFIRE

DRAGONS: WORLDS AFIRE

Published by Wizards of the Coast, Inc. FORGOTTEN REALMS, DRAGONLANCE, EBERRON, MAGIC: THE GATHERING, Wizards of the Coast, and their respective logos are trademarks of Wizards of the Coast, Inc., in the U.S.A. and other countries.

Printed in the U.S.A.

First Printing: June 2006
Library of Congress Catalog Card Number: 2006901729

9 8 7 6 5 4 3 2 1

ISBN-10: 0-7869-4166-9
ISBN-13: 978-0-7869-4166-7
620-95747720-001 EN

U.S., CANADA, ASIA, PACIFIC, & LATIN AMERICA
Wizards of the Coast, Inc.
P.O. Box 707, Renton, WA 98057-0707
+1-800-324-6496

EUROPEAN HEADQUARTERS GREAT BRITAIN
Hasbro UK Ltd
Caswell Way, Newport, Gwent NP9 0YH
Save this address for your records.

Visit our web site at www.wizards.com

AUTHORS

R.A. Salvatore

Margaret Weis and Tracy Hickman

Keith Baker

Scott McGough

COVER ARTIST

Duane O. Myers

COLOR ART

Todd Lockwood · Matt Stawicki · Michael Komarck · Greg Staples

BLACK & WHITE ART

Wayne England · Matt Stawicki · Steve Prescott · Chad Sergestketter

LINE EDITORS

Philip Athans · Patrick McGilligan · Mark Sehestedt · Susan J. Morris

ART DIRECTOR/DESIGNER

Matt Adelsperger

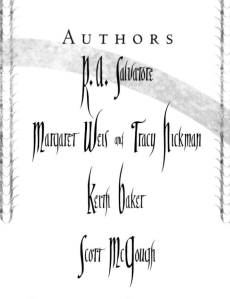

If Ever They Happened Upon My Lair

"Fill the buckets, grab a fish," muttered Ringo Heffenstone, a dwarf with exceptionally broad shoulders, even for a dwarf, and a large, square head. Ringo was quite an exception among the group of dwarves who had ventured out into the mud lands of northeastern Vaasa in that he wore no beard. A gigantic handlebar mustache, yes, but no beard. An unfortunate encounter with a gnome's fire-rocket a few years before back in the hills of northwestern Damara, the southern and more civilized neighbor to Vaasa, had left a patch of scarred skin on Ringo's chin from which no hair would sprout.

It was a sad scar for a dwarf, to be sure, but with his typical pragmatism and stoicism, Ringo had just shrugged it off and redesigned his facial hair appropriately. Nothing ever really bothered Ringo. Certainly he could grump and mutter as well as the next dwarf about present indignities, such as his current position as water mule for the troop of dwarves, but in the end everything rolled out far and wide from him, eventually toppling off his shoulders.

He came to the bank of the pond, his friends a few hundred feet behind him

by R. A. Salvatore

tipping beers and recounting their more raucous adventures with ever-increasing volume.

A burst of howling laughter made Ringo cringe and look to the south. They weren't far from Palishchuk, a city of half-orcs. They could have been there already, in fact, sleeping comfortably in a tavern. The half-orcs would gladly have taken their coin and invited them in. But though the half-orcs were no enemies of the dwarves, the troop had already decided they would avoid the Palishchukians if at all possible. Ringo and the others didn't much like the way half-orcs smelled, and even though those particular half-orcs acted far more in accordance with their human heritage than that of their orc ancestors, they still carried the peculiar aroma of their more bestial halves.

Another burst of laughter turned Ringo back to the encampment. As several of his drunken friends unsuccessfully shushed those howling loudest, Ringo shook his head.

He turned back to the pond, a vernal pool that formed every spring and summer as the frozen tundra softened. He noted the movement of some fish, flitting in and out of the shadows to the side, and shook his head again, amazed that they could survive in such an environment. If they could live through the extended Vaasan winter, in the shadow of the Great Glacier itself, how could he bring himself to catch one?

"Bah, but ye're safe, little fishies," the dwarf said to them. "Ye keep winning the good fight against this freezin' place and old Ringo ain't got no heart for killin' ye and eatin' ye."

He reached up and picked a piece of his dinner, a large bread crumb, from the left handlebar of his mustache. He'd been saving it for later, but he glanced at it and tossed it to the fish instead.

The dwarf grinned as the fish broke the surface, inhaling the crumb. Several others came up, making plopping sounds and creating interconnected rings of ripples.

Ringo watched the spectacle for a few moments then picked up one of his buckets and moved down to the water's edge. He knelt in the mud and turned the bucket sidelong in the shallows to fill it.

Just as he started to tip the bucket back upright, a wave washed in and sent water overflowing the pail, soaking the dwarf's hands and hairy forearms.

"Bah!" Ringo snorted, falling back from the freezing water.

He fell into a sitting position, facing the lake, and curled his legs to get away from the cold wash of the encroaching wave. His gaze went out to the water, where more rings widened, their eastern edges rolling in toward him.

Ringo scratched his head. It was a small pond, and little wind blew. They weren't near any hills, where a rock or a tree might have tumbled from on high. He had seen no shadow from a falling bird.

"Waves?"

The dwarf stood up and put his hands on his hips as the water calmed. A glance to the side told him that the fish were long gone.

The water stilled, and the hair on the back of Ringo's neck tingled with nervous anticipation.

"Hurry it up with that water!" one of the dwarves from the camp called.

Ringo knew he should shout a warning or turn and run back to the camp, but he stood there staring at the still water of the dark pool. The meager sunlight filtered through the clouds in the west, casting lines of lighter hue on the glassy surface.

He knew he was being watched, and that he should reach around and unfasten his heavy wooden shield and his battle-axe. He was a warrior, after all, hardened by years of adventure.

But he stood there staring. His legs would not answer his call to retreat to the camp, and his arms would not respond to his silent cries to retrieve his weapon and shield.

He saw a greater darkness beneath the flat water some distance out from shore, a blacker spot in the deep gray. The water showed no disturbance, but Ringo instinctively recognized the dark form that rose from the depths.

So smoothly that they didn't even form a ripple, a pair of horns poked up through the surface thirty feet out from the bank. The horns continued to climb into the air, five feet . . . seven . . . until between them appeared the black crown of a reptilian head.

Ringo began to tremble. His hands slid from his hips and hung loosely at his sides.

He understood what was coming, but his mind would not accept it, would not allow him to shout, run, or grab his weapon, futile as he knew that weapon to be.

The horns climbed higher, and the black head slipped gently from the water. Ringo saw the ridge of sharp scales, black as a mineshaft, framing the beast's head in armor finer than any a dwarf master smith might ever craft. Then he saw the eyes, yellow and lizardlike, and the beast paused.

The awful eyes saw him, too, he knew, and had been aware of him long before the beast had shown itself. They bored into him, framing him with their own inner light that shone as distinctively as the beam of a bull's-eye lantern.

"Hurry it up with that water!" came the call again. "I'm wantin' to drink and pee afore the night comes on."

He wanted to answer.

"Ringo?"

"Heft-the-Stone, ye dolt!" another dwarf chimed in, using the nickname they had given to their principal pack mule.

The playful insult never registered in Ringo's senses, for his thoughts were locked on those awful reptilian eyes.

Run! Ringo silently screamed, for himself and for them.

But his legs felt as if they had sunk deeply into the gripping mud. He didn't run as the water gently parted to reveal the tapering, long snout, as long as his own body but graceful and lithe. Flared nostrils came free of the water, steam rising from them. Then came the terrible maw, water running out either side between the teeth—fangs as long as the poor dwarf's leg. Weeds hung from its mouth,

9

too, caught on those great teeth, dripping as the head rose up above the gray flatness of the pond.

The beast drifted forward, slowly and silently, so that in the span of a few moments the dragon's head towered above the paralyzed dwarf, barely ten feet from the muddy bank.

Ringo's breath came in short gasps. Locked by the power of those awful reptilian eyes, his head tilted back as the head rose on the black-scaled, serpentine neck. Slowly, the dragon swayed, and Ringo moved with it, though he was totally unaware of his own motion.

Beautiful, he thought, for the grace and power of the wyrm could not be denied.

There was something preternatural, some power unbound by the limitations mere mortals might know, something godlike and beyond the sensibilities of the dwarf. Gone were any thoughts of drawing a weapon against so magnificent a beast. How could he presume to challenge a god? Who was he to even dare ask such a creature to think him worthy of battle?

Transfixed, entranced, overwhelmed by the power and the beauty, Ringo barely registered the movement, the snakelike speed of the strike as the dragon's head snapped forward, the jaws opening to fall over him.

There was darkness.

And Ringo knew no more.

"Bah, Heft-a-stone, will ye be quick about it, then?" Nordwinnil Fellhammer moaned, rising from his cross-legged position beside the campfire. "Suren that me lips are par—"

Nordwinnil's words caught in his throat as he turned to regard the pond and Ringo—or the two partial legs, knee-to-foot, standing in Ringo's boots where Ringo had just been. Nordwinnil's eyes widened and his jaw hung open as one of those legs tipped over, falling outward to plop into the mud.

"Yeah, me own throat—" said another of the dwarves, and he, too, abruptly cut off his sentence as he turned toward the pond and saw the gigantic black dragon crouching in the water near the shore,

The beast chomped down, and one of Ringo's arms fell free to splash into the pond.

"D-d-d-d-*dragon!*" Nordwinnil screamed.

He tried to sprint out to the side but turned so furiously that he twisted his legs together and wound up tumbling headlong into the tent behind him. He thrashed and scrambled as all the dwarves began to shout. He heard a thump and knew it to be an axe slapping defiantly against a wooden shield.

The ground trembled as the beast came forth from the pond, and Nordwinnil scrambled more furiously—and of course that only entangled him in the canvas all the more.

Cries assailed him, screams of fright and a growl of defiance. He heard a crossbow crank back, followed by the sharp click of the bolt's release, the hiss of the wyrm, the abbreviated shriek of the dwarf archer, and the sloppy, crackling impact of the dragon's fangs biting the dwarf in half.

Nordwinnil tucked his legs and drove forward as a rain of dwarf blood sprinkled over him and the tent. He finally came out on the far side and kept on scrambling, crawling on all fours.

He couldn't shout past the lump in his throat when he heard his companions crying out, horribly shrieking, behind him. He didn't dare look back and nearly fainted with terror when he felt a slap on his back.

But it was a dwarf, good old Pergiss MacRingle, grabbing him by the collar and dragging him along.

Good old Pergiss! Pergiss wouldn't leave him behind.

With his friend steadying him as they went, Nordwinnil managed to get his legs under him and climb to his feet. On they ran, or tried to, for the ground shook as if an earthquake had struck. The dragon stomped down on another dwarf, crushing the poor fellow into the mud. Pergiss and Nordwinnil tangled up and crashed down, and both fought to regain their footing.

Nordwinnil looked back as the dragon turned their way, and those horrible eyes found him and held him.

"Come on then, ye dolt!" Pergiss cried, but Nordwinnil couldn't move.

Pergiss looked back, and the dragon snapped its great leathery wings out wide, stealing the meager remnants of daylight with its magnificent blackness.

"By the gods," Pergiss managed to say.

The dragon's head shot forward just a few feet, its jaws opened wide, and it blew forth a spray of green-black acid.

Nordwinnil and Pergiss lifted their arms before them to fend off the deadly rain, but the sticky, burning substance engulfed them.

They screamed. They burned. They melted together so completely that anyone who happened upon the scene would never know where Nordwinnil ended and Pergiss began.

There was silence again by the still pond near Palishchuk. The buzzards watched with interest, but they dared not take wing and caw.

He was Kazmil-urshula-kelloakizilian. He was Urshula, the black wyrm of Vaasa, the Beast of the Bog, the bane of all who thought to civilize that untamable land. He had razed entire villages in his youth. He had decimated towns so completely that those who subsequently returned to the scene could not know that structures had once stood there. Tribes of goblins had paid homage to him, sacrificed to him, and carried his likeness on totems.

In his youth, those centuries before, Urshula had dominated the region from the Galena Mountains in the south and running up the eastern border to the base of the Great Glacier that described Vaasa's northern edge.

But he had grown quieter. Age had brought contentment and piles of treasure whose smell and taste—and magical energy—provided an irresistible bed for Urshula. Rarely did the dragon come forth from the soft peat and cool stones of his subterranean lair.

Every now and then, though, the smell of fresh meat, of dwarf, human, orc, or even the occasional elf, drifted down to him, and when it was accompanied by the hum of magic and the metallic taste of coins, Urshula roused.

He sat before his conquest, the dwarves all slaughtered and devoured. His forelegs, so deadly and delicate all at once, picked through the treasures as he mused whether he liked the taste of dwarf raw, as with the first kill by the lake, or acid-bathed, as with the pair to the side. A great forked tongue slipped through his fangs as he considered his options, seeking remnants of one or the other morsel to better help with his internal debate.

He soon had all of the treasure worth pilfering in a single sack. He clutched it in one claw and turned his senses to the south, from whence drifted the pungent smell of orc. Urshula wasn't really hungry any more, and the thought of sleep was inviting, but he spread his great leathery wings and lifted up high on his hind legs, his serpentine neck craning to afford him a view far to the south.

The dragon's eyes narrowed as he considered the plumes of smoke rising from the distant city. He had known of the settlement, of course, for he had heard the ruckus of its initial construction, but he had never given it much heed. The smell of orc was strong, but they were not known to be rich in either magic or coin.

The dragon looked back to the pond and considered the tunnels beneath the dark waters that would take him home. He looked back to the south and flexed his wings yet again.

Still clutching the sack, Urshula leaped into the air. Great wings rolled parallel to the ground, bent slightly, and caught the air beneath them, driving the wyrm higher. From fifty feet up he saw the city and was surprised at the size of it. Thousands of people lived there, or so it seemed, for its walls ran wide and far to the south. Scores of structures dotted the interior, some of them extensive and multi-storied.

A wave of hatred rankled the beast, and Urshula almost gave in to it and dived headlong for that intrusion. How dare they build such a place upon his land!

But then he heard the horns blowing and saw the black specks—the guards of the distant city—scrambling along the walls.

Urshula had gone against a city—not a town, but an organized and defended city—only once before. One wing, his rear right leg, and his lower torso still ached with the memory of stinging pain.

Still, the intruders could not go unpunished.

Urshula climbed higher into the darkening sky. He let forth a roar, for he wanted terror to precede his attack.

He leveled off once he passed above the clouds, and he could imagine the poor fools along the city's wall scanning the skies in desperation.

The dragon drifted south for a short while, then he dived, a power swoop that shot him out from the cloud cover at full speed, the wind shrieking over his extended wings. He heard the screams. He saw the scrambling. He smelled the tiny arrows reaching up to him.

He crossed over and strafed with his acidic breath, drawing a line of devastation down the center of the city. A few of the arrows nipped at him. One spear lifted up high enough for Urshula to bite it out of the sky.

And he was gone, out over the city's southern wall. A slight tilt of his wings angled the dragon to climb into the air once again.

Urshula knew they'd be better prepared for his second run, but there would be no second run. He rose up even higher, banked back to the north, and flew over the city from on high, well out of reach of the puny arrows.

He glided down, swooping past the remains of the dwarf camp, then dipped and plowed into the lake, lifting a wall of water high into the air.

Wings tucked back as he descended, the dragon's great body swayed to push him through the cold current of the underground river that brought water from the spring melt at the Great Glacier. Urshula would never run out of breath, though, for black dragons were perfectly adapted to such an environment. Some minutes later, the dragon turned into a side passage, a lava tube from an ancient volcano that gradually climbed so that, after a long while, he came free of the water.

He followed his subterranean network of trails unerringly, traversing corridors so wide that he could occasionally flex his wings, and so narrow that his scales scraped the worms and roots as he snaked his way through. In one of those narrow corridors, Urshula paused and sniffed. He nodded, knowing that he was parallel to his lair.

He turned his head into the soft ground and brought forth his acidic breath but sprayed it gradually, melting and loosening the dirt before him as he bored through.

He broke into the southern rim of the side chamber of his lair, crawled forth, and shook the peat and dirt from his interlocking scales. He stopped and snapped his long, thick tail against the wall of dirt, collapsing the tunnel behind him, and issued a growl that sounded almost like a cat's purr. His lamplight gaze fell over his bed of coins and gems, suits of armor and weapons. He flung his newest sack of treasure atop the pile and slithered forth.

He collapsed in pleasant thoughts of devastation and considered again the taste of dwarf, raw and cooked. His tongue snaked between his great fangs, seeking morsels and sweet memories.

Then the dragon's lamplight eyes closed, the lair fell into pitch blackness, and Kazmil-urshula-kelloakizilian, the Beast of the Bog, slept.

*   *   *

"Minor damage from a meager wyrm," said Byphast the Frozen Death. She appeared in all ways an elf, except that her hair shone silver rather than the usual golden or black, and her skin was a bit too white. Her eyes, too, did not fit the overall image, for they showed a cool shade of yellow, with a line of black centering them, like the eyes of a hunting serpent. "Palishchuk shows the scars you predicted, several years old, but they are of little consequence."

In the room was one other, seated at a small table before a trio of large bookcases, who slowly swiveled his head Byphast's way. The fabric of his gray cloak was torn in strips to reveal the velvety blackness of the robe beneath. His voluminous sleeves hung below the edge of the table, but when the man turned, his fingers showed.

Fingers of bone. A living skeleton.

Beneath the great hood of the robe, there was only blackness, and Byphast was glad for that.

Her relief did not hold, though, as Zhengyi lifted one of his skeletal hands and drew the hood back. The gray and white skull came into view. The pieces of rotting flesh and the inhuman, unearthly eyes—points of red and yellow fire—forced Byphast to glance away. And the smell, the essence of death itself, nearly backed her out of the room.

Zhengyi pulled the hood back all the way to reveal the splotches of his white hair, clumped at all angles across his bony pate. If most people coifed themselves to appear more attractive, it seemed quite apparent that Zhengyi did the opposite.

For as most people, as most creatures, reveled in life, so did Zhengyi revel in death. He had passed beyond his human form into a state of undeath. Of the many variants among the walking dead on Toril, none was more abhorrent and revolting than a lich. A vampire might charm, might even be beautiful, but a lich was not a creature of subtlety. A lich didn't enter a bargain with Death, as did a vampire. A lich wasn't an unwilling participant in the state of undeath, as were the minor skeletons, zombies, and ghouls. A lich was a purposeful creature, a wizard who by powerful enchantments and sheer force of will had defeated Death itself, had refused to surrender consciousness and self-awareness or to give in to some otherworldly, godly being.

Even Byphast the Frozen Death, the greatest white dragon of the Great Glacier, shifted uncomfortably from foot to foot in the presence of Zhengyi. She wished the corridors of Castle Perilous were wider and higher so that she might face Zhengyi in her awe-inspiring dragon form.

Realistically, though, Byphast didn't believe the lich would be impressed by even that. Certainly Zhengyi had shown no fear when he'd traversed the icy corridors of Byphast's lair to confront her in her very treasure room. He had passed through the remorhaz pit, where several of the mighty polar worms, minions of the white dragon, stood guard. He had so dominated the ice trolls Byphast used as sentries that they hadn't even warned their reptilian deity of Zhengyi's approach.

"Tell me, Byphast, what lingering damage might your own deadly breath have caused to the stone of Palishchuk?" the lich replied at last.

Byphast's eyes narrowed. Her breath was frost, of course, powerful enough to freeze solid the flesh and blood of living enemies but largely ineffective against stone.

Or against a lich.

"A black dragon's spittle is concentrated," Byphast replied, her teeth gritted. She felt a twinge of anger ripple through her elf form, screaming at her to revert to her natural state. "Black dragons can wreak devastation indeed, but in a smaller area. The breath of a white fans wider and is deadly even at the fringes. And more effective. I can kill all within without destroying the city itself. The people die, the buildings remain. Which is the wiser choice, Witch-King?"

"You know I favor you," Zhengyi replied, the meager flaps of dried skin at the corners of his mouth somehow turning up in a frozen smile.

Byphast hid her disgust. "And I am possessed of potent spells, beyond the abilities of Urshula the Black, I am sure."

"You would not wish him as an ally?"

Byphast leaned back at that, her surprise showing.

"He came forth a few years ago," Zhengyi went on, letting the question drop. "That is good. He is below that pond north of the city—of that, I am certain."

"When Zhengyi wishes to find a dragon . . ." Byphast muttered.

"I will conquer Damara, my friend. The spoils will be grand, and my dragon allies will be well rewarded."

Byphast's eyes narrowed again, and with the gleam of eagerness glowing behind them.

"Do you not think Urshula worthy of our war?" asked the lich.

"Urshula is the father of all the black dragons in the Bloodstone Lands," Byphast replied. "Enlist him and you are assured a flight of acid-spitters at your service. They are most effective at weakening a castle's walls before your ground fodder advances."

"Oh, I will enlist him," Zhengyi promised. "Remember, I have the greatest treasure of all."

Byphast's eyes flared and narrowed yet again.

He did indeed.

"Urshula is not possessed of a magical repertoire?" Zhengyi asked. He tapped a skeletal finger to the bone where his lip used to be and turned back to his small desk and the crystal ball that sat atop it.

"He is a black."

"And you are a white," Zhengyi replied, glancing back. "When first I learned of Byphast, I asked the same question of Honoringast the Red."

Byphast's eyes narrowed at the mention of the domineering red dragon, the greatest of Zhengyi's allies. Few creatures in all the world disgusted Byphast as thoroughly as did a red dragon, but she was not fool enough to test her strength and cunning against Honoringast, who was mighty even measured against his red-scaled kin. And red dragons were the most formidable of all, save the thankfully elusive, rare, and haughty golds.

" 'She is a white,' was his answer, in a tone no less dismissive than your own," Zhengyi continued. "And yet, to my great pleasure and greater gain, I later learned that you were quite skilled in the Art."

"In all the centuries, I have not heard of Urshula ever using a spell of any consequence," Byphast replied. "I have encountered him only once, at the base of the Great Glacier, and as we had both just finished devouring respective camps of fodder, we did not engage."

"You feared him?"

"Even the weakest of dragons is capable of inflicting great damage, Witch-King. It is a truism you would do well to remember."

Zhengyi's laugh sounded more as a wheeze.

"Shall I accompany you to visit Urshula?" Byphast asked as the Witch-King sat down facing the crystal ball and shrugged his cloak from his shoulders. Byphast wasn't quite sure of why he was doing that. It was her understanding that they were to travel to Urshula's lair straight away. "Or are you summoning Honoringast? Surely your arrival with a red and white at your side will intimidate Urshula more fully."

"I'll not need Honoringast, nor even Byphast," Zhengyi explained. "If Urshula is not wise enough to understand the power of spellcasting, it would not be wise to venture into his lair."

"If he has no spells then he is not as formidable as I," Byphast growled.

"True, but did you not just warn me about the weakest of dragons?"

"Yet you did not fear me?"

Zhengyi looked over at her, and she realized how ridiculous she must have seemed at that moment with her arms crossed over her chest.

"I did not fear you because I knew that you would understand the value of that which I had to offer," the lich explained. "Byphast, wise enough to engage in spells of mighty magic, was of course wise enough to recognize the greatest treasure of all. And even if you had refused my offer, you would not have been fool enough to challenge my power in that place and at that time."

"You presumed much."

"The Art requires discipline. If Urshula has not that discipline, then better that I approach him in a manner where his impetuousness can do no damage."

Zhengyi leaned over the table and peered into the crystal ball. He waved one hand over it, and a bluish-gray mist appeared inside, swirling and roiling. A moment later, the Witch-King nodded and slid his chair back. He stood up, reached into a pocket of his robe, and produced a small amethyst jewel, shaped in the form of a dragon's skull.

Byphast sucked in her breath; she knew a similar gemstone quite well.

"You have located Urshula?"

"Precisely where I said he would be," Zhengyi answered. "In a lair in the peat to the side of the vernal pool."

"You will go to him without me?"

"Pray watch," Zhengyi answered. "You may be there in spirit, at least."

As he finished, he began waving his arms slowly before him, the wide sleeves of his robes rolling hypnotically like a pair of swaying, hooded snakes. He spoke a chant, intoning the verbal components of a spell.

Byphast knew the spell, and she watched with interest as Zhengyi began to transform. Skin grew over the bones of his fingers and face. Hair sprouted from all the bare patches

on his skull, and it was not white like the clumps that already adorned his head but rich brown in hue. The white hair, too, began to darken. The robes expanded as Zhengyi grew to considerable girth, and his white grin disappeared beneath full, red lips.

He appeared as he had been in life, robust and rotund. A dark beard sprouted from his chin and jowls.

"Less of a shock, you think?" he asked.

"Urshula would try to eat either form, I am sure."

Zhengyi's laugh sounded as different from his previous wheeze as his round, fleshy form appeared different from his skeletal body. The chuckle rose up from a jiggling belly and resonated deeply in the man's thick throat.

"Shouldn't you have waited until you were near to the lair?" asked the dragon.

"Near? Why I am practically inside even as we speak."

Byphast moved up beside him as he turned to the crystal ball and began casting another spell. Looking into the ball, the dragon could see Urshula, the Beast of the Bog, curled up in his subterranean lair on a pile of treasure. She couldn't tell if it was a trick of the ball illuminating the stone and dirt walls of the chamber, or if there was some glowing lichen or other light source actually inside Urshula's home.

But it did not matter, for Byphast knew that it was no illusion. The image in the scrying ball was indeed that of Urshula and was real in time and space. Byphast turned back to regard Zhengyi just as he completed his casting.

His large body glowed for just a heartbeat then the glow broke free of his form and came forward, a translucent, glowing likeness of the man who stood behind it. It shrunk as if it had traveled a great distance away, reaching out toward the crystal ball, then disappeared inside the glass.

Urshula opened one sleepy eye, and his lamplight gaze illuminated a conical area before him. Like a spotlight, his roving eye probed the cavern. Gemstones glittered and gold gleamed as his eye's beam slipped through the shadows. The dragon's second eye popped open, and his great head snapped up when his gaze settled on a portly, bearded man, standing at ease in black velvet robes.

"Greetings, mighty Urshula," the man said.

Urshula spat at him, and the floor around the man bubbled and popped. A pile of gold melted into a single lump, and a suit of plate mail armor showed its limitations, its breastplate disintegrating under the acid breath of the black dragon.

"Impressive," the man said, glancing around him. He was unharmed, untouched, as if the acid had gone right through him.

Urshula narrowed his reptilian eyes and scrutinized the man—the *image* of a man—more closely. The dragon sensed the magic finally, and a low growl escaped through his long fangs.

"I have not come to steal from you, mighty Urshula. Nor to attack you in any way. Perhaps you have heard of me. I am Zhengyi, the Witch-King of Vaasa." The tone in his voice told the dragon that the little man thought quite highly of himself. "Ah, I see," the man went on. "My claim of kingship means little to you, no doubt, for you perceive me as one who holds claim over humans alone. Or perhaps over humans, elves, dwarves, orcs, goblins, and all the rest of the humanoid races in which you have little interest, other than to make a meal of them now and again."

The dragon increased the volume of his growl.

"But you should take note this time, Urshula, for my rise holds great implications for all who call Vaasa, or anywhere in the Bloodstone Lands, their home. I have united all the creatures of Vaasa to do battle with the feeble and foolish lords of Damara. My armies swarm south through the Galenas, and soon all the land will be mine."

"All the creatures?" Urshula replied in a voice that was both hissing and gravelly at the same time.

"For the most part."

The dragon growled.

"I am no fool," said Zhengyi. "Naturally I did not approach one as magnificent as you until I was certain that my plans would proceed. I would not enlist Urshula, the Beast of the Bog, to fight the initial battles, for I would not be worthy of such a creature as Urshula until the first victories were achieved."

"You are a fool if you think yourself worthy even then."

"Others do not agree."

"Others? Goblins and dwarves?" The dragon snorted, little puffs of black smoke popping out of his upward-facing nostrils.

"You have heard of Byphast the Frozen Death?" Zhengyi asked. The dragon's nostrils flared, and his eyes widened. "Or of Honoringast the Red?"

Urshula's head moved back at the mention of that one. The black dragon, suddenly not so sure of himself, glanced around.

"Am I now worthy?" Zhengyi asked.

Urshula lifted up to his haunches. The movement, frighteningly fast and graceful for so large a beast, had Zhengyi stepping backward despite the fact that he was just a projected image, his physical form far from the breath and bite of the black wyrm.

"If you are worthy, then you are worthy of naught but the title of fool, and no more, to disturb the rest of Urshula!" the dragon roared. "You have found my home and think yourself clever, but beware, 'Witch-King,' for none who know the home of Urshula shall live for long."

The thunder of his roaring was still reverberating off the cavern's walls when the dragon came forward. His jaws opened wide and dropped over the projected image of Zhengyi. The great dragon's teeth clamped together hard and loud right at where the lich's knees appeared. Urshula bit only insubstantial air, of course, for Zhengyi wasn't truly in the cavern, but the dragon thrashed and flailed anyway, its forelegs slapping down at that which its mouth had not bitten. And when those clawed dragon fingers passed through the insubstantial Zhengyi and slapped at the floor, Urshula flexed his great muscles and drove his iron-strong claws into the stone, raking them across, digging deep ridges.

The dragon finished by spreading wide his wings and crouching upright on his rear legs, his lamplight gaze fixed on the continuing image of the Witch-King.

"The other notable dragons of the region have joined with me," Zhengyi went on, unperturbed and apparently unimpressed. "They recognize the value and the gain of this winning campaign. When all of the Bloodstone Lands are under my command, they will be well rewarded."

"Urshula does not need others to reward him," the dragon countered. "Urshula takes what Urshula wants."

"They find security in my ranks, mighty dragon."

"Urshula kills whoever threatens Urshula."

"You are aware of the young lord gaining strength in the southland?" Zhengyi asked. "You have heard of Gareth?"

The dragon snorted.

"You know his surname, of course?"

"You have confused me with someone who would care, it seems."

" 'Dragonsbane,' " Zhengyi replied. "The young leader of those who oppose me holds the surname of Dragonsbane, and it was one earned through deeds in his rich family lines. Would he be a friend to Urshula if somehow managed to defeat me?"

"You just claimed to lead a winning campaign," the dragon reminded him.

"Indeed, and that is in no small part because of the wisdom of Byphast, Honoringast, and others who see the choice clearly."

"Then why have you disturbed my slumber? Go and win, but leave Urshula be. And consider yourself fortunate in that, for few ever leave Urshula except scattered in piles of excrement."

"Magnanimity?" Zhengyi asked as much as stated. "I offer to the dragons rewards for their assistance. I would be remiss if I did not extend the courtesy to Kazmil-urshula-kelloakizilian."

The dragon chuckled, a sound like stones being crushed by boulders in a pool of acid, and said, "You see yourself as salvation, then, as a soon-to-be-king of all you survey. I have outlived many such fools. You see yourself as one of note, but I see a pathetic human, and a dead one at that, wearing but the guise of life. Lay down, lich. Seek your kingdom and peace in a world more befitting your rotting corporeal form. Bother me no more, or I will lay you down myself."

"And if you do come against me, with or without your dragon companions," Urshula went on, "then do inform Byphast the Frozen Death that she will be the first to feel the bite of my wrath."

"You have not yet heard my offer, grand beast," Zhengyi said. He brought forth a small gem shaped like a dragon's skull. "The greatest treasure of all. Do you recognize this, Urshula?"

The dragon narrowed his eyes and issued a low growl but did not respond.

"A phylactery," Zhengyi explained. "Prepared for Urshula. I have beaten Death, mighty dragon. And I know how you might—"

"Be gone from here, abomination!" the dragon roared. "You have embraced death, not defeated it, and you only did so because you are of an inferior race, the short-lived and infirm. You presume the death of Urshula, but Urshula is older than the oldest memories of your race. And Urshula will remain when the memory of you has faded from all the world!"

The image closed its hand and slid the phylactery away. "You do not appreciate its value," Zhengyi said, then he shrugged and bowed. "Sleep well, mighty dragon. You are as impressive as I was told you would be. Perhaps another day. . . ."

"I will never see you again, else I will see you destroyed."

Urshula's words echoed and rebounded in the confined space, and it seemed as if their vibrations shook the image of Zhengyi to nothingness.

The black dragon remained crouching for some time, still as a statue, listening for any indication that Zhengyi or his minions were within the chamber or the corridors beyond.

Many hours later, the great black curled back up to sleep.

The Witch-King stood on a high, flat stone, looking north to his kingdom of Vaasa, his skeletal fingers balled into fists of rage at his sides.

The campaign had been going well He had pressed deep into Damara, conquering enemies and enlisting new allies—many of them the rotting corpses of the men his army had just slaughtered. His enemies remained divided, often too concerned with one another to pay sufficient heed to the true darkness that had come to their land.

Gareth Dragonsbane and his friends worked furiously to remedy that, to unite Damara's many lords under a single banner and stand strong against Zhengyi, but they had acted too late, so Zhengyi believed, and his victory seemed assured.

But then a small but powerful force had swept into Vaasa in his own army's wake. They had broken the siege at Palishchuk and gathered the remnants of refugees from across the wasteland into a single, formidable force. Several caravans of supplies from Castle Perilous had not reached Bloodstone Pass in the Galenas. Zhengyi's main supply route had been interrupted.

The Witch-King understood that he should not be looking north at so critical an hour. He had not the time to chase a splinter group of rebels with Gareth Dragonsbane rising to prominence before him.

"Where are you, Byphast?" he asked the cold northern breeze.

He had sent the dragon back to her glacial home with instructions to put down the rebels and their Damaran supporters, but the news coming back to him had been less than promising.

He stood there a while longer, then snapped his black robes and gray cape around him in a swift, angry turn. He strode back down the mountainside, his undead form easily gliding over the treacherous descent, and soon he walked among the rear guard of his army again, appearing once more as he had in life. The living humans who slavishly followed him would not have suffered the terrible sight of his true form.

He waited out the night in his command tent, perusing the reports and maps that were coming in from the battle fronts in the south. Truly Zhengyi's preparation for the campaign would have garnered the appreciation of the greatest generals throughout Faerûn. Information was power, Zhengyi knew, and his command tent, with its tables full of maps and miniatures of various strategic stretches of the Bloodstone Lands' terrain, and markers depicting the relative size and strength of the armies doing battle, was a testament to that knowledge. There, Zhengyi could plot his army's movements, his defensive positions, and those areas most vulnerable to attack. In that tent, the grand strategy—including the decision not to throw his weight fully against Palish-chuk—had been formulated and continually refined.

The Witch-King didn't like surprises. Despite his preparation and confidence, Zhengyi's firelight eyes often glanced back over his shoulder, to the north, in the hope of word from the white dragon. Splinter groups of powerful heroes were harder to keep track of and often more trouble than regiments of common soldiers.

The long night passed without incident. It wasn't until the next morning that Byphast, in her elf form, came walking down the trail. Zhengyi spotted her some distance off, and first sight told him that the news from the north was not good. Byphast limped, and even from a distance, she appeared more disheveled than Zhengyi had ever seen her.

The Witch-King's robes fluttered out behind him as he strode through his camp, determined to meet the white dragon on the trail beyond the hearing of his guards and soldiers.

"The rumors are true," Zhengyi said as he approached. "A band of heroes reached Palishchuk."

"To the cheers of the half-orcs," Byphast replied. "That city is more fortified than ever. Their preparations do not cease. They have thickened their walls and set out crates of stinging arrows."

Her use of that particular adjective told Zhengyi that the dragon had personally tested those defenses.

"And they have constructed greater engines of defense: catapults and ballistae that can be quickly swiveled toward the sky to strike back against airborne creatures. When I flew over the city, barbed chains rose to impede me, and I only narrowly avoided giant spears hurled my way."

"Palishchuk will be dealt with in time," Zhengyi promised.

"Without the aid of Byphast, and without any other dragons, I would guess," the white dragon replied. "The treasures of Palishchuk are not worth the risk to wing and limb."

Zhengyi nodded, still not overly concerned with the half-orc city. Once Damara had been conquered, Palishchuk would become a tiny oasis of resistance with no help forthcoming from anywhere in the Bloodstone Lands. They would not hold out for long, and Zhengyi had not yet given up hope that the half-orcs would ultimately throw in with him. They were half-orcs, after all, and would not likely be as deterred by moral issues as were the weak humans, halflings, and others of Damara.

"These heroes hid within the city?" Zhengyi asked, getting back to the problem at hand.

"Nay, they came forth quite willingly. When I escaped the chains and the spears and flew off to the north, they burst out of Palishchuk's gate in pursuit."

"And you killed them?"

Byphast's twisted expression gave him the answer before the dragon began to speak. "They are accompanied by mighty wizards and priests. Their knights glow with wards to defeat my deadly breath, and their armor sings with magic to deter the rake of my claws."

"A small band?"

"Fifty strong, and well designed to do battle with dragons."

"Byphast would not normally flee from such a group." Zhengyi did nothing to keep the contempt out of his voice, nor from his expression, as he narrowed his eyes and sneered.

"If forced to do battle with them—if ever they happened upon my lair—then I would surely destroy them," the dragon replied without hesitation. "But scars would accompany that win, I am sure, and in that place, at this time, they were not worth the trouble."

"You serve Zhengyi." Even as the Witch-King took the conversation in that direction, Byphast's statement, "if ever they happened upon my lair," resonated in his thoughts.

"I agreed to fight beside Zhengyi's forces," the dragon replied. "I did not agree to wage such battles alone in the bogs of Vaasa."

Zhengyi produced a phylactery, the one to which Byphast had attuned herself. If the dragon was slain, her energy and life-force would transfer to the phylactery, and she would become undead, a dracolich.

"You forget?" the lich said.

"It is a final safeguard, but not one I am anxious to use. If in the course of events I am slain, then so be it. That is the risk my kind need take whenever we come forth into the world of lesser creatures. But I'll not chase after the undeath you offer."

"Ah, Byphast, it is a piteous thing to see a creature of your reputation reduced to such fear."

Lizardlike eyes narrowed, and a low growl escaped the dragon's elf lips.

"Very well, then," said Zhengyi. "I will deal with the intruders myself. I'll not have them nipping at my heels all the way through Damara. Go and rejoin the commanders at the front. Lay waste to the foolish Damarans who stand in our way."

Byphast didn't move, nor did her expression change from the hateful look she shot Zhengyi's way.

If that threat bothered the Witch-King at all, though, he didn't show it. He turned his back on the wyrm in elf's clothing and stalked back to his vast encampment.

"Donegan!" cried Maryin Felspur, Knight of the Order.

"*Sir* Donegan," the senior knight corrected. He walked his armor-clad horse out from the ranks, the heavy hooves making plopping sounds as the fifteen-hundred-pound steed, with three hundred pounds of armor and two hundred pounds of rider, crossed the soft, wet ground. Donegan paced right up to Maryin, the only female knight of the ten who had come out from Lord Gareth's ranks in Damara, accompanying more than fifty footsoldiers, half a dozen priests, and a trio of annoying wizards.

"Sir Donegan," Maryin corrected herself with outward humility.

She didn't have her helmet on, though, and her smile betrayed her tone. Serving as scout for the group, the lithe Maryin was the least armored of the knights, and her horse, a fine, strong young pinto, barely larger than a pony, wore only protective breast- and faceplates. Maryin preferred the bow and used her speed to skirt the edges of the encounters with Zhengyi's minions, thinning their ranks at advantageous points so that Donegan and Sir Bevell could best exploit their enemies.

Donegan did not dismount. His mail of interlocking plates made such movements tedious, particularly in trying to get back up onto the nearly eighteen-hand charger. Instead he leaned over as far as his encumbering suit would allow and lifted the visor of his helmet.

Maryin crouched beside a depression, a tear in the ground that was half-filled with brown water.

"Only a creature the size of a dragon could make such an imprint," Maryin said.

Donegan straightened and scanned the area. He noted a second and third imprint behind and several more ahead but beyond that, nothing.

"Master Fisticus," he called to the leader of the trio of wizards, "pray you and your companions ready your components and our shielding spells. These tracks are not old, and it would appear that the wyrm has taken to the air. It could swoop upon us from on high at any time, and I'll not have its deadly breath decimating our ranks before we've had a chance to engage the beast."

"Perhaps we should slide back toward Palishchuk, my lord," Maryin offered quietly. "In reach of their ballistae—"

"Nay," Sir Donegan began before Maryin had even finished. "The wyrm is too smart to be goaded near the town again. The half-orcs nearly brought it down the first time."

"If it is the same dragon."

That thought gave Donegan pause, for he could not dismiss the reasoning. Until a few months ago, Donegan had seen only one dragon in all of his twenty years of adventuring, and that was a small white up near the Great Glacier. With the coming of Zhengyi, the Knight of the Order had learned far more than ever he had intended regarding dragonkind, for evil chromatic wyrms of many colors filled the sky above the Witch-King's advance. Reds and whites had laid waste to many villages, including Donegan's home town, and the knight had done battle with a pair of blues, an encounter that had cost him a horse and had left a blackened line of lightning scarring across the back of his otherwise silvery armor.

Too many dragons, Donegan thought. Far too many dragons. . . .

***

Zhengyi stood on the northeastern bank of a small pond a few miles to the north of Palishchuk. Gone were the human trappings of his former self; he saw no need for such vanities out there, alone. He had his hood back, revealing his skull, the splotchy patches of hair, and the flaps of rotting skin. His robes smelled of mildew, hanging in tatters and showing green spots of mold. He clutched a twisted oaken staff, leaning on it heavily, and stared out to the south.

He saw their approach, the glint of the sun off their lance tips, off the armor of their mounts. He heard the thunder of hooves and marching soldiers.

The remnants of the Witch-King's lips curled in a wicked smile. He thought of Byphast's declaration: that she would not go against such a force except in her lair.

Any dragon would fight against any odds to protect its lair. To the death.

More flashes showed in the south. They followed the trail Zhengyi had dug with his magic, thinking it the tracks of a dragon.

He lifted his twisted oaken staff again, located a suitable spot, and uttered a command word. The ground erupted where he'd pointed his staff. Clumps of dirt flew into the air. The magic dug at the soft ground, bursts of energy tore up and threw aside yards of earth as efficiently and powerfully as a dragon's talons might.

Zhengyi glanced southeast, to the distant troop of warriors. Perhaps they had noted the disturbance, perhaps not. They would be there soon enough, in any case. His spell completed, the deep hole dug, Zhengyi stepped into the water. It did not feel cold to the Witch-King, of course, for he could no longer experience any such sensations. In any case, no chill was more profound than the icy embrace of death.

His robes floated out behind him as he stepped in deeper, and soon he was under the water, not breathing, not moving. As the surface stilled, Zhengyi's otherworldly eyes peered through the film to the northeastern bank. His trail would take them to the dig. He clutched the staff more tightly, preparing his next spell.

Maryin crept along the muddy ground, staying low and letting her elven cloak, a garment of magical camouflage, hang down around her. She had left her horse back with Donegan and the others, who marched along some hundred feet behind her. Maryin's job was to detect any potential ambushes, and to keep them moving toward the dragon. Given the dirt flying high into the air a few moments earlier, the knight had every reason to believe she had completed that task.

She had found another few tracks not far back, for the beast had apparently set down, but then she came upon a great hole, not far from the bank of a small pond. She crouched at the rim, considering the tunnel at the bottom.

"Did you go to ground, wyrm?" she whispered under her breath.

Maryin lingered for a few moments, then hearing the approach of her companions she straightened, glanced around, and moved her hand out from under the protection of her cloak, raising her fist high into the air.

She glanced at the water, not realizing that the eyes of the Witch-King looked back at her. Behind her, Sir Donegan slowed his contingent and approached with some caution. He walked his horse up beside the knight scout.

"Into the tunnel?" he asked, inspecting the hole. "Or is it a ruse, and the beast has gone under the pond?"

Maryin pulled back her cowl and shrugged. "I'm finding nothing to say it is and nothing to say it isn't."

"A wonderful scout you are."

Maryin smiled at him. "I can track almost anything, and you know it well—even that little lass who thought to sneak into your room. But you cannot expect me to track a dragon that keeps taking to the sky. Do you think its beating wings will flatten grass from on high? Do you think the beast will cut a wake through the land as a boat might do across a lake?"

Sir Donegan laughed at her endless sarcasm and the wicked little jab against him. He still had a bone to pick with Maryin over that wench incident, for Donegan had been anticipating the visit, and the interception had not been appreciated. But that was a fight for another day, and a thought came to him.

"Has the water risen?"

Maryin looked at him, curious, then caught on and moved to the pond's bank where she began inspecting for signs of a recent swell. The pond wasn't very large, after all, and surely the displacement would be noticeable in the event a creature as large as a dragon had entered its depths.

A moment later, Maryin stood straight again and shook her head.

"And so the wyrm did not enter the pond," Donegan said with a sigh. "Good enough, then."

There are no tracks from the hole to the water, and if the beast had taken to the air for any distance, we should have seen it—or should have heard the splash when it dived in. My guess is that the dragon, confident and oblivious to our pursuit, took to the tun—"

She hunched forward, and Donegan leaped back. Behind them, horses and soldiers bristled. From the hole came a low, throaty growl, a resonating rumble befitting a beast of a dragon's stature.

"Form up!" Sir Donegan commanded.

He turned his charger and thundered back to the ranks. Maryin pulled her cowl back over her head and face and appeared to melt into the shadows at the pool's edge.

The growl continued for a few moments, then gradually receded

Lances were lowered, swords were drawn, and wizards and priests prepared their spells.

Then it was quiet once more. And through the long hush, no great monster sprang from the hole.

When Donegan and the others finally dared to approach, they stood on the edge of the deep, wide, funnel-shaped pit, looking to the broad tunnel at its base, which ran off both east and west.

"It would seem that we have found our wyrm," Sir Donegan told his troop.

"Are we certain that a dragon dug this pit?" another knight asked.

"There are spells that can facilitate such things," Fisticus the wizard replied. "As there are beasts. . . ."

"A dragon?"

"There is little turmoil a dragon cannot create," Fisticus explained. "Such a wyrm as the one that attacked Palishchuk those days ago would have little trouble boring through the soft ground of the Vaasan summer."

Sir Gavaland, another Knight of the Order, said, "One would think that if the dragon meant to announce its presence in such a manner, it would have burst forth to attack us in that moment of surprise."

"If it knew we were here," Donegan replied.

"The growl?"

"A purr of satisfaction before settling down to sleep?" the wizard offered. "Such beasts are known to growl as often as a man might sigh or yawn."

"Pray it is a yawn, then," said Donegan, "and one announcing that the beast is ready for a long and sound nap." He looked around at his soldiers, grinning from ear to ear beneath his upraised visor. "One from which it will never awaken."

That brought a host of nods and grins from the rank and file.

Off to the side, Maryin neither nodded or grinned. She knew what was coming, and what her role would be, before Sir Donegan even motioned to her to enter the pit. It occurred to her that perhaps she would do well to don her heavier plate mail and hire an elf to handle the scouting.

⁂

Under the water, Zhengyi nodded with contentment as he watched the troop disappear over the pit's rim. His spell mimicking the dragon's roar had been well placed through use of his complimentary enchantment of ventriloquism, or so it would seem.

The Witch-King knew that he should be away at once—back to the south and Damara, where the battle raged—but he lingered a bit longer in the pond, and when all of the soldiers had gone into the pit save those few left to guard the horses, he emerged again on the northeastern bank.

The three fools standing with the horses still stared at the pit, oblivious to the danger, when the Witch-King came calling.

⁂

She knew that her elven cloak could protect her from prying eyes, but still Maryin felt vulnerable as she edged her way down the enormous tunnel—certainly high and wide enough for a dragon to charge through it. Lichen covered the walls, emitting a soft light, like starlight in a forest clearing. Though thankful for that illumination—for it meant she had to carry no torch—at the same time she feared the glow might make her just as plain to the wyrm's clever eyes.

She felt the beast's presence before she smelled or heard it, a pervasive aura of fear that hung in the air.

Maryin went down to all fours and crawled along. No retreat would be fast enough if the beast spotted her, so her only hope lay in not being detected at all.

She rounded a bend and held her breath as she peered into a distant chamber. There it was, and it was not the beast that had recently attacked Palishchuk. For even in the dim light, she could see that its scales glistened black, not white.

She retreated slowly for some time, inching out backward. Then she turned and ran, two hundred yards or more up the tunnel, to where Donegan and the others waited, including the armored horses of the knights Donegan and Bevell.

"A large black," she explained in as soft a voice as possible while she drew the chamber's layout for them in a patch of soft dirt.

Fisticus and the other wizards went to work, coordinating the spells they would need to fend off the acidic breath of a black dragon.

"A white would present fewer challenges," the lead wizard complained. "Our spells to defeat its freezing breath are more specialized and complete."

"Perhaps I can borrow some fence paint and change the beast's color while it sleeps," came Maryin's sarcastic reply.

"That would be helpful," Fisticus shot back without hesitation.

"Enough," Donegan scolded them both. "Black dragons are comparable to whites—at least it's not an ancient red awaiting us."

"We have spells specifically to defeat the fiery breath of a—" Fisticus began.

"And any red worth its scales would have mighty spells to dwarf your own," Donegan interrupted. "In this case we need only defeat the black's initial spray and get our forces in close. Once by its side, we will take the beast down quickly."

Fisticus nodded and moved to stand next to Maryin's map. "The distance from the tunnel to the beast?" he asked. "And where in the approach are we likely to be engaged?"

Getting into the heart of the dragon's lair was little challenge for the Witch-King. In his two-dimensional shadow form, Zhengyi merely slipped into a crack in the stone and slithered his way down. He stood off to the side of the main floor, not far from Urshula but concealed by the nature of his form, and by other enchantments, so that the dragon did not sense him.

He watched with great amusement as the stealthy female knight crept back down again to observe the dragon. A pair of wizards followed, magically shielded and hidden.

"Pathetic," Zhengyi mouthed under his breath.

He raised his bony hand and added an illusion—from the dragon's perspective—to further hide the intruders, for he did not want Urshula to detect the approaching force too soon.

The wizards cast their spell and hustled away, and as he considered their creation, Zhengyi had to admit their cleverness. Nodding, he knew what was coming next. He waved his hand again, and his illusion disappeared.

Urshula's eye opened just a bit, and Zhengyi watched the muscles along the dragon's great forelegs tighten with readiness. Down the tunnel came the warriors in a sudden charge, weapons and armor clattering.

Urshula sprang into a crouch, his great horned head swiveling in line.

Zhengyi marveled that the soldiers did not break ranks. Not one of them fled from the sight of a great dragon. Glad he was that he had come back to the dragon's lair, for the fortitude of the troop or knights could not be underestimated.

Urshula crouched back, and Zhengyi felt the beast's rumbling inhalation, the preparation for its first devastating strike. The warriors did not slow, approaching the place where the wizards had set their enchantment. Urshula's neck shot forward, his jaws opening wide, a cone of acidic spittle bursting forth.

It hit a barrier—a solid, impenetrable wall of magical force—and spattered and sizzled. Only a bit of it splashed over the wall, sting-ing a few of the warriors. But their charge was not slowed. They parted and flowed around the edges of the magical barrier in perfect unison. On the near side, their troop flowed back together, guided by the armored knights, and closed in on the confused dragon.

Urshula reared and lifted his head high—and was promptly engulfed by a fireball, then a second and a third before he could even react. And when he ducked back down, the warriors were there, slashing, stabbing, and hacking away with abandon. They filtered around the wyrm, cheering and shouting, trying to overwhelm the beast with sudden and brutal fury.

But Urshula was a dragon, after all, the beast of beasts. A sudden frenzy of stamping legs, raking claws, swiping tail, and battering wings quickly stole the advantage.

One knight stood above the fray, barking out orders, lifting his sword high and calling for the warriors to rally around him.

The dragon's maw closed over him to the waist, and lifted him high for all to see. Warriors cried out for him as his armored legs thrashed helplessly.

Urshula clamped down, and the knight's lower torso dropped to the floor. The rest came flying free as well, when Urshula snapped his head around. The knight served as a missile to crash through several ranks of warriors. Those who fell farthest aside proved the fortunate ones for the time being, though, for the armored missile was fast followed by a second blast of acid.

Men melted and died.

Before he could begin to applaud the wyrm, Zhengyi looked around to see a barrage of energy bolts—green, blue, and violet—swarming the dragon's way. Urshula's victory roar became a cry of pain as the bolts burned into him, stabbing through scales that could not protect the beast from such attacks.

The dragon spotted the wizards, grouped inside the tunnel entrance just to the left. Ignoring the stabs from the warriors still thrashing as his sides, Urshula spat again.

Stones all around the wizards sizzled and popped, but the three were protected. One did wince in pain, though he still managed to join his companions in the next missile barrage.

Zhengyi, fearing that the dragon would be overwhelmed too quickly, thought he should intervene.

But Urshula reared up on his hind legs and spread wide his wings. He beat them furiously, lifting dust, coins, and pebbles from the floor to fly at the distant wizards. The debris did no real damage, but it prevented any further casting—and more importantly, Zhengyi realized, it made clear the limits of their magical shielding.

"Brilliant," the Witch-King applauded.

The dragon's reaction was not a surprise to Sir Donegan. Trained by Gareth Dragonsbane himself—a man who had well-earned his surname—Donegan had designed the attack in four specific phases: First, the defeat of the beast's initial killing breath; second, the charge; third, a barrage of magic that should force the dragon's attention away from the last, most deadly part.

The knights Donegan and Bevell sat on their horses back up the tunnel awaiting the dragon's reaction. As it reared, they spurred their mounts to charge. Lances lowered, the two skilled knights swerved left and right around the magical wall of force, rejoined on the far side of the barrier, and thundered in together at the still-oblivious dragon.

They caught the beast side-by-side in the belly, the weakest point of a dragon's natural armor. With the weight of their huge steeds driving them on, and the enchantments placed upon those lances, the weapons struck home, cracking through the hard shell of scales and driving deep into the beast's soft innards.

Down came the roaring beast. But Donegan and Bevell were already moving, turning their mounts aside and leaving their lances quivering in the dragon's belly. As one, the skilled knights drew forth swords from over their shoulders. Bevell's broadsword flared with fire at his silent command, while Donegan brought forth a two-handed blade that gleamed with an inner, magical light. As the dragon's wing descended over him, Donegan clenched his legs tightly and thrust his weapon up with both hands. The beast howled again and retracted.

Bevell found less success against the opposite wing, and though he landed a solid slash, the limb buffeted him and sent him tumbling from his mount and sprawling to the floor.

"Rally to me!" Donegan called his warriors, and those still capable of battle did just that.

The dragon spun to face him, and Donegan nearly swooned, thinking the moment of his death at hand.

But the wizards struck again. A fireball engulfed the beast's head, and a host of magical missiles disappeared into the flaming sphere.

Donegan used the moment to charge his rushing mount in hard against the dragon's side. He dismounted and slapped his horse away, then took up his sword in both hands and drove a mighty slash against the beast's scales. All around him, his warriors cheered and attacked, stabbing and hacking with abandon.

The dragon was hurt; the beast swayed.

"Be done with it!" Sir Donegan cried, thinking the moment of victory upon them.

But the dragon spun, its tail flying across, slapping Donegan and the others aside, launching them across the stone and dirt floor.

The knight tried to rise. His helm had turned, stealing his vision, and his sword had flown from his grasp. He fumbled around before a hand grabbed his shoulder and steadied him.

He adjusted his helm and saw Maryin grinning at him and nodding. She handed him his sword.

"Let us be done with this," she said.

Zhengyi enjoyed the spectacle. He marveled at the troop's preparation and fortitude. Few men could stand so long in the face of an angry wyrm. Impressive, too, was Urshula's resilience and ferocity.

But the dragon was sorely wounded, the Witch-King realized. One of the lances had snapped off, and blood poured from the hole—and no doubt the remaining lance head tore at the creature's insides.

And those wizards came on again, relentless, their fireballs and energy bolts taking a heavy toll.

Zhengyi had come to serve as an equalizer, but surprised he was to find that it was Urshula, and not the humans, who needed his efforts. He could not allow it to be so easy for them.

The Witch-King slipped back into his shadow form and slid into a crack in the wall.

"Fire, this time," Fisticus the wizard told his two companions. "When the wyrm lifts high its head, engulf it."

All three wizards readied their spells, watching intently as Fisticus determined the pattern of the dragon's movements.

"One . . ." he counted, "two . . ."

"Do say 'three,'" a raspy voice behind the trio interrupted.

Zhengyi watched the trio stiffen, and he grinned as he imagined the expressions on their faces. He didn't let that distract him, though, as he began casting his favorite spell.

The wizards whirled around, right in the face of a sudden burst of intertwined multicolored beams of shimmering light.

Fisticus threw his arm up before his eyes while the wizard to his left was bathed in blue. That unfortunate man, blinded by the brilliance of Zhengyi's spell, tried to scream, but his skin hardened to stone, and he froze in place with his mouth agape.

Purple light engulfed Fisticus, and he was gone—just gone, removed from the Prime Material Plane and launched randomly through the multiverse, though at least his abrupt departure allowed him to avoid the blast of lightning that jolted and seared the man to his right. The bolt arced through where Fisticus had been standing and crackled against the wizard statue across the way. The solid rock he had become

exploded under the pressure of the lightning, sending finger pebbles and elbow rocks flying.

And a second hue washed over the wizard who had borne the initial shock of the lightning strike. Already down and near death, he mustered all of his remaining energy for one final shriek of agony as a red glow washed over him and he erupted in flames. He couldn't even manage to roll on the floor, however, so he just lay there burning.

Zhengyi gave a raspy sigh and shook his head.

"Appreciation, dear Urshula?" he whispered as he turned his attention back to the dragon and the larger fight, to find that his intrusion had not gone unnoticed.

"The Witch-King!" one man yelled.

At the dragon's side, Sir Donegan grimaced at the thought that such a foe had come against them at so desperate a time. He could only pray that his soldier was wrong and could only hope that they could be done with the beast quickly.

"Fisticus, finish it!" he yelled as he struck his great sword again against the dragon's flank.

He managed a roll as he completed the strike to gain a view of the wizards—or of what remained of them. Donegan took note of a shadowy figure against the stone, but he couldn't pause long enough to consider it at any length.

"Fight on, my warriors! The wyrm is failing!" he cried, rallying his troops and throwing himself with abandon against the great beast.

Urshula heard that claim, and couldn't rightly dismiss it. The wizards' strikes had wounded him badly, and he could feel the tip of a lance rattling around beneath his scaly armor, tearing up his insides.

"Zhengyi? My ally?" Urshula grumbled in the course of his continuing growl, and he was glad indeed to see one of the wizards smoldering on the floor, and the remaining piece of a second standing as stone, blasted to nothingness from the waist up.

But where was Zhengyi?

A sting in Urshula's side brought him from his contemplation and reminded him of his immediate concerns. He thrashed and stomped a man flat with his hind leg then battered down with his wing, knocking aside several others. His tail whipped out the other way, driving back yet another group of the stubborn warriors.

Zhengyi watched patiently from within a crack in the stone, the material components for several spells ready in hand. He silently applauded Urshula's ferocity as the dragon scooped up a man in his jaws and crunched him flat. Then the dragon snapped his head and let fly the human missile, bowling several men over.

In that instant, Zhengyi thought the dragon might prevail.

But Urshula lurched to the side, and Zhengyi spied the great knight who had struck the devastating blow. Urshula tried to turn on the man, too, but a second warrior, the same female scout Zhengyi had first seen enter the dragon's lair, had cunningly made her way to the dragon's back and up his neck. When the distracted wyrm focused on the knight, she drove a slender sword under the back of the dragon's skull.

Zhengyi shook his head and produced the dragon skull phylactery.

"Witch-King!" Urshula bellowed in a great voice that echoed through the chamber.

Then the wyrm reminded Zhengyi and all of the others exactly why dragons were so rightly feared. Urshula leaped up, snapping his head back, forward, then down. The motion flipped the female warrior right over the crown of the dragon's head spikes so violently that she could never have held on. The fall from twenty feet to the stone might have killed her, but the dragon never let it get that far. Biting out, his jaws covered her so that her head, feet, and one flailing arm fell free from her body.

And through all of that, the dragon continued his leap and mid-air roll. Urshula's size became his primary weapon as he crashed down atop the bulk of the remaining force, crushing them under his great weight.

33

Zhengyi grimaced as the black dragon's eyes tightened in pain, for that attack forced weapons and ridges of armor through the dragon's scales, injuring him badly as he crushed and thrashed the life from many of his enemies.

But not from the resourceful and valiant knight with the huge sword, Zhengyi saw, as that man danced out from under the tumbling wyrm and spun, slashing hard at the dragon's flailing foreleg then moving past the limb to stab hard at the beast's torso.

But before his blade met scales, an invisible force grabbed at the knight, the hand of telekinesis. As he leaped at the wyrm, he rose up over the beast and climbed into the air.

Zhengyi, quite pleased with himself, kept the man climbing.

＊＊＊

Sir Donegan whipped around with great ferocity, trying to break free of the magical grasp. Rage gripped him as surely as the dragon's spell as he saw again and again that image of the great wyrm biting Maryin apart. He went up twenty feet, fifty feet, and more, helpless as the dragon continued to slaughter his warriors, many of whom stared up at their flying leader, mouths hanging open, hope flying from their widened eyes.

Donegan slashed his great sword, as if trying to cut through some physical hand, but there was nothing to hit.

The knight turned his attention to the ceiling, which he fast approached. He braced himself for the impact, but never quite got there.

The invisible force let him go.

Screaming and cursing as he dropped, Sir Donegan refused to accept his fate. His startled cry became a roar of defiance, and he twisted himself around, lining his sword up with the head of the dragon, who did not see him coming.

Donegan's blade drove in against the beast's skull, cracking through the bone. Donegan held on until he, too, smashed head first into the wyrm. His helmet jolted down, cracking his collarbone at either side. His neck compacted so forcefully that his spine turned to powder. He crunched into place and held for a moment then twisted over backward.

He rolled away, off the wyrm, whose great head was held suspended in the air, Donegan's sword quivering in place like a third horn.

＊＊＊

"Witch-King?" Urshula bellowed again, in a voice bubbling with blood. He peered at the wall where the wizards had been felled, and red filled his vision. "Witch-King!"

And Zhengyi answered him, not physically, but telepathically. Urshula spied a dark tunnel before him, and at its end, in bright light, stood the lich, holding the small dragon skull phylactery. Urshula instinctively resisted the pull of it. But there, in Zhengyi's outstretched hand, was the promise of life, where otherwise there was only death. In that moment of terror, the blackness of oblivion looming, the wyrm surrendered to Zhengyi.

Urshula's spirit flew from his dying body and rushed down the tunnel into the dragon skull gem.

Zhengyi marveled at his prize, for the skull glowed bright, seething with the spirit energy of the trapped dragon soul, the newborn dracolich Urshula.

Zhengyi's newfound ally.

The Witch-King lowered the gem and considered the scene. He had timed his intervention perfectly, for only a couple of the warriors remained alive, and they lay helpless, squirming, groaning, and bleeding on the floor.

Zhengyi didn't offer them the courtesy of a quick death. He cast another spell and magically departed with his prize taken and his victory complete, leaving them to their slow, painful deaths.

"You thought you had won those months ago when you defeated the force that had slipped behind you into Vaasa," Byphast scolded Zhengyi on a cold Damaran winter morning.

"I won the day, indeed," the Witch-King replied, and he looked up from the great tome on his desk to regard the dragon in elf form.

"My kin are fleeing you," Byphast went on. "Lord Dragonsbane is a foe we will not face again. The allies arrayed against you are more formidable than you believed."

"But they are mortal," Zhengyi corrected. "And soon enough they will grow feeble with age and will wither and die."

"You believed your kingdom secured," the dragon countered.

Zhengyi had to refrain from laughing at her, so shaken did she seem by his calm demeanor. For her observations were correct; it was indeed all crumbling around him, and he knew that well. Gareth Dragonsbane could quite possibly win the day in Damara, and in that event the paladin would, at the very least, drive Zhengyi into hiding in a dark hole in Vaasa.

"It amuses me to see a dragon so fretful and obsessed with the near future," he replied.

"Your plan will fail!"

"My plan will sleep. Cannot a dragon, a creature who might raze a town and retire comfortably in her lair for a century or more, understand the concept of patience? You disappoint me, Byphast. Do you not understand that while our enemies are mortal, I am not? And neither are you," he reminded her, nodding to the shelf beside his desk where several gemstone dragon skulls sat waiting for the spirits of their attuned wyrms.

"My power comes not from my physical form," the Witch-King continued, "but from the blackness that resides in the hearts of all men."

He slipped his hands under the covers of the great tome and lifted it just a bit, just enough for Byphast to note the black binding engraved with brands of dragons—rearing dragons, sitting dragons, sleeping dragons, fighting dragons. Zhengyi eased the book back down, reached into his belt pouch, and produced a glowing dragon skull gem.

"Urshula the Black," Byphast remarked.

Zhengyi placed the skull against the center of the opened tome and whispered a few arcane words as he pressed down upon it.

The skull sank into the pages, disappearing within the depths of the tome.

Byphast sucked in her breath and stared hard at the Witch-King.

"If I do not win now, I win later," Zhengyi explained. "With my allies beside me. Some foolish human, elf, or other mortal creature will find this tome and will seek the power contained within. In so doing he will unleash Urshula in his greater form."

Zhengyi paused and glanced behind him, drawing Byphast's gaze to a huge bookcase full of similar books.

"His greed, his frailty, his secret desire—nay, desperation—to grasp this great treasure that only I can offer him, will perpetuate my grand schemes, whatever the outcome of the coming battles on the fields of Damara."

"So confident. . . ." Byphast said with a shake of her head and a smile that came from pity.

"Do you seek to sever your bond with the phylactery?" Zhengyi asked. "Do you wish to abandon this gift of immortality that I have offered you?"

Byphast's smile withered.

"I thought not," said Zhengyi. He closed the great book and lifted it into place on the shelf behind him. "My power is as eternal as a reasoning being's fear of death, Byphast. Thus, I am eternal." He glanced back at the newly finished tome. "Urshula was defeated in his lair, slain by the knights of the Bloodstone Army. But that only made him stronger, as King Gareth, or his descendants, will one day learn."

Byphast stood very still for some time, soaking it all in. "I will not continue the fight," she decided. "I will return to the Great Glacier and my distant home."

Zhengyi shrugged as if it did not matter—and at that time, it really did not.

"But you will not sever your bond with the phylactery," he noted.

Byphast stiffened and squared her jaw. "I will live another thousand years," she declared.

But Zhengyi only smiled and said, "So be it. I am patient."

About the Author

R.A. Salvatore was born in Massachusetts in 1959. His love affair with fantasy, and with literature in general, began during his sophomore year of college when he was given a copy of J.R.R. Tolkien's *The Lord of the Rings* as a Christmas gift. He promptly changed his major from computer science to journalism. He received a Bachelor of Science Degree in Communications in 1981, then returned for the degree he always cherished, the Bachelor of Arts in English. He began writing seriously in 1982, penning the manuscript that would become *Echoes of the Fourth Magic.*

His first published novel was *The Crystal Shard* from TSR in 1988 and he is still best known as the creator of the dark elf Drizzt, one of fantasy's most beloved characters.

His novel *The Silent Blade* won the Origins Award, and in the fall of 1997, his letters, manuscripts, and other professional papers were donated to the R.A. Salvatore Library at his alma mater, Fitchburg State College in Fitchburg, Massachusetts.

About the Artist

When **Todd Lockwood** attended his first Science Fiction and Fantasy convention, in Winnipeg, Ontario, a door was opened that would lead to a staff position at TSR, the makers of the popular role-playing game DUNGEONS & DRAGONS. Over the next seven years, he built an impressive body of fantasy images, and helped to redefine the look of the popular DUNGEONS & DRAGONS game for the Third Edition release.

His work has been honored with multiple appearances in *Spectrum* and the *Communication Arts Illustration Annual*, twelve Chesleys, two prestigious World Fantasy Art Show awards, and numerous industry awards. Now he finds himself, his wife, and three children in Washington state, freelancing again, but doing the kind of work he enjoys, with fans all over the planet. His first art book, *Transitions*, from Chrysalis books (UK), was released in September of 2003. You can see more of his work at his website, www.toddlockwood.com.

here be dragons

{A KENDER TALE}

Tasslehoff Burrfoot was having a bad day. This was something new for the kender. Humans have bad days all the time. So do ogres and goblins and even elves, on occasion. Kender do not. Good days are a kender's birthright, ranking right up there with lock picks (because the world would be a much friendlier place if everyone would simply share what they owned!) and wanderlust (because what's the point of having a world if you don't see as much of it as possible?). Thus, Tasslehoff was not prepared to handle a bad day. He simply did not know what to do. Which is what led him to the cave with the dragon.

But we're getting ahead of the story.

The bad day started when Tasslehoff—all four-some feet of him, with his topknot of brown hair tastefully decorated with a sprightly sunflower, and wearing a green jacket and his favorite purple pants with the gold splotches—arrived at the walled city of Pigeon Falls, located west of the city of Barter near the River Swift in the foothills of the Highguard mountain range on the continent

by Margaret Weis and Tracy Hickman

of Ansalon in the world of Krynn. The city of Pigeon Falls was small—it was noted on only one of the seven maps currently in Tasslehoff's possession—but he paid it a visit because the name, Pigeon Falls, intrigued him.

Sitting beneath a tree outside the city walls, the kender looked the city over and thought that it was a shame Pigeon Falls wasn't on every single one of his maps, for it deserved to be. The city was small, but prosperous. The stone wall that encircled and protected the city was tall and formidable and in good repair. Fertile farm lands surrounded the walls.

The War of the Lance (which had ended only a few years previous) and the deprivations caused by the Dark Queen's dragons, who had devastated many cities in Abanasinia, had apparently left this small city unscathed.

Tasslehoff did not immediately enter Pigeon Falls, but sat at his ease beneath the tree, watching those who came and went. He noted that the guards at the gate stopped everyone who wanted to go inside the city walls. Tas was too far away to hear what they were saying, but he guessed from long experience that the guards were asking people in a friendly way what their business was in the city. The guards were jovial, teasing the young women who came driving geese to market, exchanging jests with the farmers on their carts, and bowing respectfully to wealthy merchants.

Tas had never seen such friendly gate guards and he thought he might try entering the city by the gate, something unusual for kender, who know from sad experience that even the friendliest guards turn immediately

unfriendly when confronted by a kender. Why this was so was beyond Tasslehoff, though it had been explained to him many times by his dear old friend the dwarf, Flint Fireforge.

"It's because you can't keep your hands out of other people's pockets," Flint told Tas grumpily.

Tas brought a picture of the old dwarf to mind. Shorter than the kender, but stockier in build, the dwarf would go all red in the face and his beard quiver and his eyes nearly disappear in the crinkles that came when he scrunched up his eyebrows to yell at the kender. Tas missed Flint a great deal.

"I never put my hand in someone else's pocket in my life!" Tasslehoff protested indignantly.

"What's this?" Flint held up his thumb.

"Your thumb, Flint," said Tasslehoff, wondering why his friend was changing the subject.

"And what do I usually wear on this thumb?" the dwarf demanded angrily.

Tas hazarded a guess. "A golden ring?"

"And where is my golden ring?" Flint scowled at him.

"I don't know, Flint," said Tas. "Did you lose it?" He was concerned.

Flint reached out, took hold of Tasslehoff's hand and thrust it in the kender's face. He pointed. "What's that?"

"My thumb," said Tasslehoff, mystified.

"And what is on your thumb?"

Tas looked. He was amazed. He honestly had no recollection of having seen it before now. "A golden ring!"

The ring was too big for him and wobbled a bit, but he thought it looked well on him.

"It's just like yours, Flint," Tas said, pleased.

"That's because it *is* mine!" the irate dwarf bellowed.

"Is it?" Tas was pleased. "There! You thought you'd lost it and I found it for you. You must have dropped it."

"Bosh!" Flint seized hold of the ring and snatched it off the kender's thumb. He shook the ring under Tasslehoff's nose. "This is why city guards with any sense never allow kender inside their gates!"

"Because we find things people have lost?" Tas was understandably confused.

"Because you can't keep your hands out of people's pockets!" Flint roared.

"The ring wasn't in your pocket, Flint," Tasslehoff felt called upon to point out. "It was on my thumb. Like I said, you must have dropped it . . ."

At that point Flint stomped off, the conversation ended, and Tasslehoff never did find out why gate guards were so narrow-minded.

Perhaps these guards would be different.

Hope springing eternal in Tas's breast, he smartened himself up. He carefully combed the long topknot of hair that flowed down from the top of his head. He brushed off his bright purple trousers and straightened his green shirt and arranged all the bags and pouches that were slung over various parts of his body to their best advantage. Said bags and pouches contained all the kender's worldly goods.

Tas had no idea what was in his pouches, for, like most kender, any object he "found" seemed the most wonderful and valuable object in the world (be it emerald ring or bird's nest), something he would keep forever (a petrified frog), and he promptly forgot about it the moment he dropped it inside his pouch (how did that frog come to be petrified?). This made life a constant happy surprise for Tasslehoff, who was always finding the most marvelous and unexpected things every time he put his hand in his pouch.

Tugging up his orange stockings, Tas strolled down the hill and politely took his place at the end of the line. He soon found himself right up at the front, this due to the fact that whenever the person in front of him glanced around and saw a kender standing behind him, that person immediately stepped out of line.

"You can go ahead," the person would say, gesturing with one hand and holding the other hand tightly over whatever valuables he or she possessed.

41

"Why, thank you," Tasslehoff would say, charmed, and he would move up a notch. He really liked the people of Pigeon Falls.

The next thing he knew, he was standing before the gate guard.

"Hullo," said Tasslehoff Burrfoot cheerily, "I've come to Pigeon Falls to see the falling pigeons."

The guard took one look at him. "No kender."

"But I've never seen a falling pig—"

"No kender."

"It's just that—"

"No kender!" The guard emphasized his statement with a prod in the kender's stomach from a very sharp spear.

"Ouch," said Tasslehoff, and rubbing his maltreated stomach, he took his diminutive self sadly back to his tree.

It appeared that if he wanted to visit the town of Pigeon Falls, he would have to find some quiet and unobtrusive way to sneak inside.

A farmer and a hay cart provided the perfect opportunity. Tasslehoff could not only ride inside the town in comfort, he could take a little snooze at the same time. The kender gave the farmer a friendly wave, waited until the man had driven past him, then swiftly and nimbly ran down the hill, climbed up onto the cart, burrowed his way inside the fragrant hay, and closed his eyes. The cart rumbled over the bumpy road and the soothing motion lulled the kender to sleep.

The next thing Tas knew, he was being rudely stabbed in the backside by a pitch fork.

"Ouch!" he yelped.

"Ah, ha!" said a nasty voice. "I thought I'd find you trying to sneak in!"

A large hand reached inside the mound of hay, clapped itself over Tasslehoff's belt, dragged him out, and dumped him unceremoniously on the ground.

"No kender," said the gate guard, glaring. He made a threatening gesture with the pitchfork. "We don't like kender in Pigeon Falls! Be gone with you!"

"Ferret-face," Tas muttered, though only to himself.

Plucking hay out of his hair, he went back to sit under his tree. He hoped the falling pigeons were worth all this trouble, but he was beginning to doubt it.

Seeing as how he wasn't likely to get in through the gate, Tas decided to take a little stroll around the outside of the city wall to locate some other way he might enter. As luck would have it, he found a drainage pipe that penetrated the wall. The pipe carried off rain water that collected in the streets and dumped it (and whatever else it picked up) into the river.

The only drawback to this was that the drainage pipe was fitted with an iron grate. This proved only a minor impediment. Tasslehoff brought out his lock pick tools and, first making certain that none of the guards walking around on top of the wall could see him, he set to work. In moments, the iron grate lay on the ground and the kender was crawling up the drain pipe.

Emerging, he washed off the muck as best

he could in a horse trough, then set off to the see the sights.

"Excuse me, Mistress," said Tasslehoff, walking into a baker's shop, "I'm here to see the falling pigeons—"

The woman gave a shriek of fury that reminded Tasslehoff of one of Lord Soth's banshees. She (the woman, not the banshee) picked up a broom, ran around the counter, and began smacking Tas over the head.

"Be gone!" *Thwack!*

"But, ma'am, I'm only—"

"Be gone with you!" *Thwack, thwack!*

"It's just that I've never seen—"

"We don't like kender!" *Thwack, thwack, slam*—the slam being where the woman shoved him out the door and slammed it shut on him.

Her shrieks roused the populace. Once in the street, Tas was set upon by other shopkeepers wielding various instruments of destruction, from brooms to shovels to clubs and, in the case of the butcher, a dead chicken.

Tas was saved from the onslaught by the self-same gate guard, who had been on his way home to dinner when he heard the commotion. He picked up the kender by the seat of his britches and the collar of his shirt, hauled him to the front gate, and tossed him headlong out into the dusty road.

"No kender!" the guard bellowed.

Tasslehoff stood up, brushed himself off, wiped the dead chicken juice out of his eyes, and yelled, "I didn't want to see your stupid pigeons fall anyway!"

He was walking along the road, looking at this and that and everything and nothing, and thinking that this was probably the worst day of his life, when his sharp kender eyes saw, off in the distance, what appeared to be a cave.

Caves draw kender like flames draw moths. The thought that there might be something living in the cave, or that there might be treasure in the cave, or both together, is irresistible to kender. Tas immediately turned his footsteps in that direction.

He discovered right off that he wasn't the first person to do this. He came upon a trail scored with deep wagon ruts. The trail was old and unused, for weeds were growing in the wagon ruts. But Tas could see that heavily laden wagons had traveled back and forth across it for some time. The kender was excited. Not only was this a cave, it was a mine!

He imagined those wagons laden with gold or silver or maybe even iron ore to be turned into steel, then the most valuable commodity on Krynn. No wonder the town of Pigeon Falls had appeared to be so prosperous.

He continued following the trail, speculating on what might have happened to end the mining. Perhaps there had been a collapse or the mine had run out of ore, or . . .

And then there was the answer right in front of him on a wooden sign on a stake that had been hammered into the ground.

WARNING!
MINE CLOSED!
HERE BE DRAGONS!

"How exciting!" exclaimed Tasslehoff Burrfoot. His bad day had turned good. "This is definitely better than pigeons."

He kept going, picking up his pace.

Tasslehoff passed by several more signs on his way to the cave, all of them announcing that *here be dragons*. This was, of course, meant as a warning to stay away and would have been taken as such by most people, but kender are not most people. Besides being extremely curious, kender are utterly fearless—a volatile combination, as anyone who has ever adventured with a kender (and managed to survive) will tell you.

Not that kender are foolhardy. Tasslehoff did not think of himself as jauntily walking into the jaws (literally) of death. His friend, Tanis Half-Elven, was always encouraging Tas to consider if a proposed action by the kender was "conducive to long life". Tas did consider this, though he generally ended up doing what he wanted to anyway.

On this occasion, his thinking went something along these lines: "Yes, there's a dragon, and dragons are extremely dangerous and not at all conducive to long life, but the dragon is probably out. I'll just look over his treasure horde a bit and see if I come across anything interesting." Or: "The dragon will probably be sleeping. They do sleep a lot, you know. I'll just look over his treasure horde a bit and see if I come across anything interesting."

There was always the possibility that the dragon might be in and he might be awake, but Tas considered the odds of that pretty low (one in three). And if the dragon *was* there and he *was* awake and in a bad mood and decided to eat the kender, well, there had never yet been a kender who died peacefully in his bed of old age. Tasslehoff had no intention of being the first.

As stated, Tas was not foolhardy. Arriving at the mouth of the cave, he did not immediately charge inside. He stopped to look about for signs of recent dragon activity—scales sparkling in the dirt, enormous footprints, scorch marks on the walls, etc. He saw nothing. He cocked an ear and listened for sounds of a dragon. Dragons always had stentorian breathing (whatever a stentorian was; Tas thought it might be some sort of whistle). He listened for sounds of a large creature shuffling about, stomping its feet, lashing its tail. He heard nothing. He sniffed the air for the scent of brimstone, but he didn't smell anything, either.

44

WARNING MINE HERE BE DRAGONS!

"I wonder if he moved?" Tasslehoff asked himself, disappointed. It seemed his bad day was going to continue. Everyone knew that when a dragon moved, he took his treasure with him.

The mouth of the cave was large and opened into an even larger chamber, so large that, peering up, Tas could not see the ceiling. Dusk was making the cave dusky and, the next thing Tas knew, a swarm of bats flew down around him, wheeling and dodging, flying off to find dinner. Tas ducked his head to keep the bats from mussing his topknot and thought glumly that here was another sign that the dragon had departed. No self-respecting dragon shares his cave with bats.

Tas almost turned back, but then decided that since he'd come all this way, he might as well explore a bit. After all, he could possibly come across the odd jewel-encrusted chalice the dragon had accidentally left behind. Or there might be a bugbear living here. While not as good as a dragon, a bugbear was better than nothing.

Tas continued on and his perseverance was rewarded. He made a wonderful discovery. Several very fine brass lanterns had been left at the opening of a mining shaft. The lanterns were neatly arranged on the cavern floor and they had apparently been here awhile, for they were covered with dust and bat droppings. Tas, who had neglected to bring a torch, was pleased. He did wonder, as he picked up one of the lanterns and examined it, who could have left such expensive lanterns here and why they hadn't come back to retrieve them. The most obvious answer was that the owners had all died horribly in the mine, but Tas chose to take the optimistic view that they had been so loaded up with treasure they had no room in their wagon.

A rummage through several pouches produced not one tinderbox, but three. He also found several candles. He placed one in the lantern and had it lighted in no time. Lantern in hand, he continued on his way down the mine shaft.

The shaft sloped downhill at a steep angle. He occasionally passed carts that had once been loaded with ore, but which were now loaded with bat droppings.

He kept walking.

The shaft went on a for a long way without ever seeming to get to where it was going, and he had to admit that it did not appear to be leading to a dragon or even a bugbear. Tas stopped every so often to look and listen and sniff and smell nothing. He was starting to grow discouraged and bored and was rummaging in his pouch for something to eat, when his light glinted off metal.

Tas found a piece of armor—a grieve or some such thing—that had been discarded, probably due to a broken strap. The armor was covered in dust. Tas picked it up and brushed it off. Like the lanterns, the piece of armor was of fine quality. Tas stuffed it in one of his pouches and kept going. Here was a puzzle.

Armor meant knights. Knights traipsing about an abandoned mine meant they were likely hunting the dragon. But the dragon-hunting knights had apparently not slain the dragon, otherwise they would have removed the signs warning HERE BE DRAGONS. (Or at least put up a sign that said HERE *NOT* BE DRAGONS.) The logical conclusion was that the dragon had been the winner. But, in that case, where was the dragon? Hence, the puzzle.

Tas continued going down the mine shaft. The candle burned so low he had to replace it, and still he kept going. Then, about half way through the next candle, the shaft made a sharp turn and suddenly deposited Tasslehoff in a huge chamber that was amazingly (considering it was a couple of miles underground) brightly lit.

Tasslehoff almost dropped his lantern and stared, astonished. He was more astonished than he'd ever been in his life and that was saying something, considering that he'd traveled back in time with Caramon, and visited the Abyss with the Dark Queen and taken a flying citadel out for a spin, and done a lot of other truly astonishing things. He'd never seen anything like this, however.

The floor of the chamber was covered with knights—all of them dead. Tas did not have to look twice to see they were dead, for the knights were nothing but steel and bone. Some of the dead knights had lances or spears in their bony hands. Others had swords. Tas didn't know what had killed them, but he figured it was probably the dragon—the large blue dragon that was glaring down on him from high up above him.

The very fierce large blue dragon.

"Hullo, up there," said Tasslehoff and he gave a little gulp. He wasn't afraid, mind you. Just startled.

The dragon didn't answer. Which was rude. Even for a dragon.

Tas stared up at it and realized suddenly that it was a very fierce looking blue dragon who wasn't moving. His blue wings were outspread and his jaws open so that his fangs and sharp teeth gleamed in the light. His enormous claws were flexed, ready to rip apart his foe. His blue scales glinted as he was about to dive. But he wasn't diving or biting or ripping. The dragon was just hanging there in mid air, in mid snarl, glaring down at Tasslehoff with bright gleaming eyes. Directly underneath the dragon was the dragon's treasure, all in a huge mound on the floor, glittering and shining and sparkling in the light.

"I wonder how he does that," Tasslehoff said, craning his neck to view the dragon.

He waited several moments to see if the dragon would leap or flap or dive or blast lightning bolts at him or do *something*.

The dragon continued to just hang there, suspended, glaring at him.

Tasslehoff's neck started to get a crick in it. He lowered his head and rubbed his neck, and right there before him was the answer to one of his questions—the source of the bright light.

A dead wizard.

The wizard's corpse, clad in white robes that must have once been quite sumptuous, but which were now moth- and mouse-eaten (not to mention the blood stains), was propped up against a wall. In the dead hand was a staff and the bright light was beaming from a large crystal atop the staff.

Tasslehoff felt a tingling in his fingertips that spread to his hands and all the way up his arms and into his head. That magical staff with its magical light was the most wonderful thing he'd ever seen. Caramon's twin brother Raistlin had owned a magical staff. Tasslehoff had always longed to examine Raistlin's staff, but the wizard had threatened to turn him into a cricket and feed him to a frog if he'd so much as touched his pinky finger to it. And while being a cricket might be interesting, being fed to a frog didn't hold much appeal, and so between that and the fact that Raistlin never let the staff out of his sight, Tas had never had a chance to study it.

Here was his opportunity.

Tasslehoff didn't think this wizard would mind if he touched the staff, since the wizard was pretty much past the point of minding anything.

Ignoring the dragon's treasure (after all, if you've seen one diamond the size of your fist, you've seen them all), Tas hurried over to look at the staff.

The light shining from the crystal was so bright that Tas had to squint to look at it. He reached out his hand, wrapped his fingers around the smooth wooden staff, and carefully and gently lifted it out of the wizard's bony grasp.

At that moment, a great many things happened.

First, the light on top of the staff went out.

Second, there came an enormous crash as of something extremely heavy falling from a great height.

Third, he heard silence, followed by a pain-filled groan, followed by an angry snarl.

"Oops," said Tasslehoff Burrfoot.

Now, those who have adventured in company with a kender will tell you that "oops" is the single most terrible word ever heard coming from a kender's lips. (For many, it's the last word they ever hear.) "Oops" means the kender has made a mistake. And though kender are very small people, they generally make very large mistakes.

This was one of them.

It did occur to Tasslehoff the moment he touched the staff that perhaps the staff's magic was responsible for keeping the dragon suspended in mid-air and that by touching the staff he would disrupt the spell. Since he was touching the staff at the time, this notion came to him too late to do any good.

And, as it turned out, his notion was right. Touching the staff disrupted the spell and freed the dragon, who came crashing down to the ground, right on top of his treasure horde.

Tasslehoff thought fast.

"Oh, hullo, there!" he said cheerily, peering into the darkness and locating the dragon. "It's me. Tasslehoff Burrfoot. Hero of the Lance." He mentioned this in modest tones, then added quickly, "I saved you from the evil wizard who had put a spell on you. No need to thank me. I'll just be going now. Good-bye!"

Tas's lantern was by the opening of the chamber where he'd almost dropped it. Putting down the staff, so that the dragon wouldn't mistake him for a wizard, Tasslehoff starting walking rapidly toward the exit.

An enormous blue-scaled paw slammed down on the floor right in front of him.

"Not so fast," snarled the dragon.

Tas squinched shut his eyes, thinking he was going to be eaten. Then, figuring if he was going to be eaten by a dragon, that was a sight he wouldn't want to miss, he opened his eyes again.

The dragon did not appear as though he about to eat him. Instead, the dragon lowered his massive head until he was only a few feet from Tas and looked at him straight in the eye. The dragon's own eyes glinted in the light of Tas's lantern.

The dragon asked a most unexpected question.

"Um . . . do you know me?" The dragon winced, as though in pain.

"I beg your pardon?" said Tasslehoff, not sure if this was a trick question. Everyone knew that dragons sometimes asked trick questions that you had to answer correctly if you wanted to keep from being eaten. "I'm not sure exactly what you mean."

"You said you saved me from a wizard," the dragon continued gruffly. He sounded embarrassed. "That implies that you and I have some sort of relationship . . ."

Now the only relationship that came to Tas's mind was that of "eater" and "eatee", but he wisely did not mention this.

"I'm sorry," said Tas. "I'm afraid I don't understand. Perhaps if you could explain it to me."

As he was speaking, the kender tried to sidle his way around the enormous paw.

The dragon rumbled in his blue chest and shifted about uncomfortably on top of the pile of treasure. "It's just that . . . I must have hit my head when I fell, because . . . it's the damndest thing . . . but I can't seem to recall my own name."

"You can't?" Tasslehoff asked, so amazed he came to a stop.

"No, nothing." The dragon sounded glum. "And I've got a beastly headache. Do you happen to know . . . uh . . . my name?"

"George," said Tasslehoff promptly. George had always been one of his favorite names and so few people were called George nowadays.

"George," the dragon repeated. "Are you sure? George doesn't seem the right sort of name for a dragon."

"Oh." Tas was disappointed. "You know you're a dragon, do you?"

"Well, of course!" The dragon snapped. "I may have a large bump on my head, but I'm not an idiot. A gully dwarf could see that I'm a dragon!"

Tas had to admit that the wings, the tail, the fangs, and the blue scales did sort of give that away.

"And you are a kender," the dragon continued. He added in a dour voice, "I seem to recall that as a rule I don't like kender."

"That was until you met me," said Tasslehoff brightly. He had his plan all worked out now. "You see, we're partners. Partners in crime. We're thieves."

"Thieves?" the dragon repeated, astounded.

"Two of the greatest thieves Krynn has ever known," said Tas, who was now enjoying himself. He sat down on a large chest of gold bars and made himself comfortable. "You and I are notorious throughout Ansalon. Why"—he waved his hand—"just look at the loot we've accumulated!"

"This is . . . ours?" The dragon was awed. He stared around at the golden plates and the chests of steel coins and the jeweled crowns and diadems and scepters covered with pearls and lots of other objects too fabulous and numerous to be described.

"Yes, all ours," Tas replied proudly.

"I'm a thief," the dragon said, mulling this over. "I pick locks and sneak into houses—"

"You're the second-story man," Tas explained. "You sneak into the windows on the second story."

"I appear be rather large to do that," the dragon countered.

"But that's the very reason why! I'm too short to be the second-story man, so I'm the first-story man. I pick the locks on the front door. You're tall, so you crawl in the windows. You're ever so stealthy."

"I am?" The dragon was skeptical. "Stealthy?"

"The most stealthy dragon in Krynn."

The dragon appeared to think about this, but thinking evidently caused him pain, for he winced again. He glanced about at the dead knights. "So, what happened here? Looks like some sort of battle took place."

"Oh, it was very exciting! We were down here in our cave, taking inventory, when we were rudely set upon by these knights and their wizard," Tas said. "We fought valiantly, especially myself. Did I tell you I was a Hero of the Lance? Anyway, the wizard cast a spell on you that caused you to be suspended from the ceiling. I wrestled with him and managed to take away his staff, and I freed you and here we are. Now, as I was just on my way out, I can go fetch something for that headache of yours."

Tas started to edge his way toward the exit once more.

"Wait!" The dragon shifted his paw, blocking Tas's escape route. He peered intently at the corpses. "These knights have been dead a long time. So has the wizard. A long, long time."

Tas looked at one of the corpses holding a sword in its bony hand and was forced to concede that the dragon had a point. The dragon's eyes narrowed. Clearly, he was starting to grow suspicious.

"Undead!" exclaimed Tas, inspired. "Skeletal warriors. Led by a skeletal wizard. It was a desperate battle against the forces of the evil god of Undeath, Chemosh, but we were victorious."

Tas mopped his brow with his shirt sleeve. All this thinking was starting to wear on him.

"You can see where you blasted the undead with your lightning breath," Tas pointed out, indicating scorch marks on the floor and walls. "And here's where you back-stabbed a knight. He never knew what hit him."

"But what would undead want with treasure?" the dragon asked.

Tas was beginning to believe being eaten would be less trouble. "Look, George, I wasn't going to tell you this. I didn't want to worry you. But, the truth is, the undead were sent to assassinate us. We have a rival—Ragar the Ugly."

Admittedly the name didn't sound all that impressive, but Tas was fast running out of inspiration.

"Ragar sent these undead to finish us off."

"Where is this Ragar the Ugly?" the dragon demanded grimly. "We should deal with him."

"He's back in his hideout—Castle Ugly. It's a really long way from here and, frankly, you're not up to it, George. Really, you're not. I'm going to go out to get a soothing poultice for you to put on your head. Doesn't that sound nice? Tomorrow we'll deal with Ragar."

"Soothing poultice," the dragon reflected. "Yes, that does sound good. Something cooling."

"You just lie down and rest a bit. Take it easy. There's a city not far from here. I'll just pop into the apothecary, borrow . . . er . . . steal a poultice, and be right back."

"I think I will rest," said the dragon and he brushed aside a skeleton or two to clear a space. "Don't be gone long . . . Er, forgive me, friend, but what is your name?"

"Igor," said Tasslehoff, another of his favorite names. "Igor the Merciless." He was actually quite pleased by his new name.

"Don't be gone long, Igor," said the dragon, and he closed his eyes and winced as he gingerly laid his massive head down on the treasure pile.

Tas darted over to his lantern, picked it up, and glanced back at the dragon. The creature did truly have a very nasty swelling, about the size of a house, on its head. The dragon gave a groan and burrowed down more comfortably into the treasure.

Tas waited no longer. He dashed out of the chamber and into the corridor and never stopped until he was standing, puffing, by one of the signs that said HERE BE DRAGONS.

"A truer word was never spoken," said Tasslehoff, and he gave the sign a pat.

Being a little weary from all that hard thinking, he decided that what he really needed was a good sleep in a good bed in a good inn. He made his way beneath the starlit sky—he guessed it must be about the middle of the night—and walked back to the town of Pigeon Falls.

As good fortune would have it, he came across a small gate in the wall that he'd missed the first time around. The gate led out to the path that went to the river. His lock pick tools were never far from hand and Tasslehoff had the small gate open in seconds.

He found an inn that looked nice, went around back, jimmied open a window and let himself in (so as not wake up the owner).

Once inside, he absent-mindedly pocketed several pieces of cutlery that were lying about on a table, rummaged around in a few drawers, went through the belongings of the slumbering guests, and slipped a few interesting items into his pouches. Then, yawning, he found a bed that wasn't being used, tucked himself in, said his prayers, and closed his eyes.

"I'd make a really great thief," Igor the Merciless reflected as he was drifting off. "It's a good thing for society that I'm a hero."

The next thing Tasslehoff knew, a noise as of a ton of bricks falling down, accompanied by a terrified scream, hoisted him right out of his bed. The tumbling bricks and the scream were followed by a lot more screams and, added to that, came shouts and bellow-ings, the ringing of bells and blowing of horns and beating of drums.

"It can't be a parade," said Tas groggily. "It's the middle of the night."

The inhabitants of the inn were running about in their night clothes, peering out the window and demanding to know what in the Abyss was going on.

"Dragon!" someone yelled from outside. Torch lights flared. "A blue dragon is attacking the city!"

"Oops," said Tasslehoff Burrfoot.

Of course, it could be some other blue dragon who just happened to be wandering by, but he had the sinking feeling it wasn't.

One of the guests, a mercenary warrior, was raving that he couldn't find his sword. It had been right on the floor beside him as he lay sleeping and now it was gone.

"Here it is," said Tasslehoff, handing it over. "You dropped it."

The warrior glared at him, snatched up his sword—never saying thank you—and raced out of the inn. The other guests decided to remain inside the inn, mostly crawling under the beds and heavy articles of furniture. The owner, dashing off to the wine cellar to make certain the dragon didn't get into the best wine, caught a glimpse of Tas, skidded to a halt, and came dashing back.

51

"What is a filth of a kender doing in my inn?" the owner roared. "What is a filth of a kender doing in my city?"

Outside, Tasslehoff could hear the shouts and the screams and bellowings growing louder and, over that, the call to arms.

Tasslehoff drew himself up straight and tall. He fixed the inn's owner with a steely eye. "I'm dealing with the dragon," he said.

And he walked resolutely and courageously out into the street.

Sure enough, there was George. The dragon's blue scales showed up quite well in the light of hundreds of torches. The dragon's legs squashed flat one section of the town wall. His front claw thrust clear through a wall on the second floor of a large house, smashing woodwork and plaster and glass. His tail knocked over a guard tower, so that the tower hung at a precarious angle, with the guards jumping for their lives.

Roused by the alarm, the citizens of Pigeon Falls were armed for battle with weapons of all varieties, from swords to pitchforks to rolling pins. Fortunately, battle had not yet been joined. Although the captain of the town militia was exhorting his men to charge, most were overcome by dragonfear and were hiding behind buildings, clutching their weapons in shaking hands, and staring open-mouthed and white-faced at the dragon.

The dragon, meanwhile, had just managed to extricate his claw from the second story of the house—bringing down the roof as he did so—and was staring about in growing rage.

Tasslehoff Burrfoot heaved a sigh. He shoved and wriggled his way through the terror-stricken crowd and came to stand alone in the middle of the town square.

The crowd went "oooh" and "aaah," and the people fell all over themselves backing up to give the kender more room. Someone did mutter, "How did a kender get into town?" but several voices shushed him.

The dragon looked down accusingly at Tasslehoff.

"You didn't come back."

"I'm sorry," said Tas meekly. "I fell asleep. It was a tiring battle. All those skeletal warriors . . . and all."

He wasn't feeling very chipper. It was obvious that the dragon had recovered somewhat and was having second, third, and probably fourth thoughts about Tasslehoff's story. There is no telling what would have happened if, at that moment, some fool hadn't fired off one of the catapults. A largish rock sailed through the air and hit the dragon smack in the middle of its forehead.

The dragon reeled and, in that moment, remembered everything.

~⁂~

Thunderbolt (the dragon's real name) remembered the knights (who had been quite alive at the time) and that blasted white robed wizard invading his snug cave. He recalled the battle and how he'd breathed his deadly lightning breath on the knights and picked them up in his jaws and flung them back to the ground. He recalled gobs of blood and the sweet screams of the dying and the lovely sound of breaking bones. Finally, he recalled the immense satisfaction he felt as skewered that wizard in his gut with a claw. The wizard slumped down the wall. He was bleeding profusely, but he was still conscious, blast him, and he was able to get off a last magic spell—waving his staff and chanting.

Thunderbolt remembered being blinded by white light and then suddenly everything—including time—ground to a halt. When the dragon could see again, he discovered that he was hanging in mid-air, wings extended, jaws open, claws stretched to kill, and he was stuck this way. Suspended, held prisoner in time and space. And the wizard who had cast the foul spell died before he could uncast it.

Years passed. Thunderbolt didn't know how many. He was frozen in his cave and he couldn't get free. He might have to hang this way for all eternity. He had nearly given up hope of ever being found when the kender had appeared inside his chamber.

This kender. The one standing right in front of him. The kender who had touched the wizard's staff and freed the dragon.

True, Thunderbolt knew, the kender had not done so on purpose. The kender had freed him accidentally. Then he'd lied to the dragon, making up that folderol about being a thief, a kender tale that had led the dazed and headachy and befuddled dragon to try his hand at thieving, with the result that he

was now in peril of his life, not to mention looking utterly ridiculous.

Tasslehoff saw the dragon blink with pain. Then the dragon's eyes opened wide and then narrowed to slits and then the large blue dragon glared down at the kender.

Tas realized in that moment that the dragon's amnesia was cured. The dragon remembered everything. Tas knew this by the glint in the dragon's now focused eyes and the barring of his fangs.

"Well, it's been a good life," Tasslehoff said to himself, as he waited to be eaten. "Too bad it couldn't have lasted longer, but that's the way Otik's spiced potatoes crumble."

The dragon lifted a powerful claw . . .

. . . and handed Tas a jeweled necklace.

"I found this," said the dragon. "You must have dropped it."

Tasslehoff was struck speechless for the first, last, and only time in his life that he could recall at this particular moment. He bent down and picked up the necklace.

"I'll just be leaving now," said the dragon.

He shifted his enormous body around, completing the ruin of the guard tower and destroying a few more sections of wall as he attempted to extricate himself. He walked off.

"Cease fire!" the captain of the militia yelled, though no one had fired or was about to fire, except the man at the catapult and, as it turned out, he'd fainted from terror and fallen on top of the triggering mechanism.

Thus ended the attack of the blue dragon on the city of Pigeon Falls.

Thunderbolt returned to his cave. On his way, he smashed every one of the HERE BE DRAGONS sign. By Takhisis, no wonder those confounded knights had discovered him! Might as well list him in the tourist guides!

As he returned to his comfortable cave, Thunderbolt reflected on his actions. He could have eaten the kender, should have eaten the kender. But the kender *had* saved him from that cruel spell and, besides, Thunderbolt was forced to admit, he had always kind of liked the name George.

So few dragons were named George nowadays.

Tasslehoff Burrfoot was now not only a Hero of the Lance, he was also the Hero of Pigeon Falls. People crowded around him, slapping him on the back. They hoisted him onto their shoulders and carried him through the streets of town. They gave him the key to the city, which he really didn't need, due to the lock picks, and threw a banquet in his honor.

He was urged to make a speech, which he did.

"Thank you," he said, "but really all I wanted was to see the pigeons fall."

Then it was explained to him that it was water falls not pigeon falls that gave the town its name. The falls were named for the pigeons, which Tas thought was pretty lame. He didn't say so, however. Heroes are always polite.

After his speech, he was hugged by the Lord Mayor's wife, who was a large-bosomed, stout woman. It was at this point that Tasslehoff remembered there were other cities to see, other caves to visit, other dragons to outwit.

So Tasslehoff Burrfoot, Hero of the Lance and of Pigeon Falls, left this part of Krynn, never to return there again.

If he had, he would have seen new signs posted all around the city—just in case any wandering dragons happened to be passing by.

WARNING TO DRAGONS!
HERE BE KENDER!

And from that day to this, kender have always been welcome in Pigeon Falls.

About the Authors

Margaret Weis and Tracy Hickman have been writing best-selling DRAGONLANCE novels for over twenty years. Together, they have written over thirty novels, in all; in addition they have written solo fiction, graphic novels, and role-playing games, edited multiple collections of stories, and contributed to numerous game products.

Born in Missouri, **Margaret Weis** graduated from the University of Missouri, Columbia, and started out with publishing houses in Missouri, writing and editing juvenile fiction, before coming to TSR in Lake Geneva, Wisconsin, as an editor, in 1983. She first teamed up as a writer, with Hickman, in 1984, co-authoring the Dragonlance Chronicles trilogy, which became the first of many of their books to be listed as a *New York Times* best-seller. They followed their first collaboration up with the Dragonlance Legends trilogy in 1985. These series, set in the fantasy world of Krynn, have sold over twenty million copies worldwide, and have been translated and published in twenty foreign countries.

The primary narrative of the Dragonlance saga is contained in Legends and Chronicles, and the subsequent Weis and Hickman books *The Second Generation* (a collection of novellas), *Dragons of Summer Flame*, and The War of Souls Trilogy.

Weis and Hickman have also edited numerous novels by other TSR/Wizards authors exploring the rich history and world of DRAGONLANCE. They have edited multiple anthologies of DRAGONLANCE short stories, including the one containing their own short stories, *Dragons in the Archives: The Best of Weis and Hickman*. They continue to edit and contribute to numerous DRAGONLANCE game products and specialty volumes such as *The Art of Dragonlance*, *Leaves of the Inn of the Last Home*, and DRAGONLANCE Sourcebooks.

Weis has also written the DRAGONLANCE books *Brothers in Arms*, *The Doom Brigade*, and *Draconian Measures*. Under her sole byline, Weis has written *The Soulforge* about the childhood and youth of Raistlin Majere, and she is currently writing the ongoing Dark Disciple Trilogy, which features Mina, the lead character of the War of Souls Trilogy.

Outside of DRAGONLANCE and away from TSR/Wizards of the Coast, Weis has written the Mag Force 7 novels *Knights of the Black Earth, Robot Blues,* and *Hung Out;* she wrote *Dark Heart,* with her son, David Baldwin; and she is currently writing a paranormal romance novel with her daughter, Elizabeth Baldwin.

Also as a solo author, Weis has written the Star of the Guardian galactic fantasy saga, and the Dragonvarld Trilogy. She is owner of Sovereign Press, the publisher of the new DRAGONLANCE D20 RPG products licensed by Wizards of the Coast, and owner of Margaret Weis Productions, publisher of the role-playing game based on the film, *Serenity,* by Joss Whedon.

Born in Salt Lake City, Utah, **Tracy Hickman** spent two years as a missionary for the Church of Jesus Christ of Latter Day Saints (the Mormons), before becoming a game designer. He has been designing role-playing fantasy-world games for twenty-five years. He joined TSR in 1983 and served as a leader of the team that created the DRAGONLANCE world. Besides the DRAGONLANCE novels he has also co-authored the following best-selling books with Weis: The Darksword Trilogy, The Rose of the Prophet Trilogy, The Death's Gate Cycle (seven book series), The Sovereign Stone Trllogy, and The Starshield series.

Hickman has designed many non-DRAGONLANCE game products and written extensively for different game worlds. He has also written solo novels and books with other writing partners. His novels as a solo author include *The Immortals, Requiem of Stars,* and STARCRAFT: *Speed of Darkness.* With his wife Laura Curtis Hickman, also a co-creator of the DRAGONLANCE world, Hickman is writing the ongoing Bronze Canticles series.

Nowadays Hickman lives in Utah, and Weis lives in Wisconsin, but they continue their longtime close collaboration on the upcoming Dark Chronicles, an unofficial sequel to Legends, long-awaited by their fans, revealing untold Dragonlance tales from the original epic. The first instalment of the new trilogy is due to be published in 2006.

About the Artist

Matt Stawicki was born and raised in the Delaware area. He attended the Pennsylvania School of Art and Design and graduated in 1991. Since beginning his professional career in 1992, he has created many images for a wide range of products and clients including video gamecovers, collectible card images, book covers, collectors plates and fantasy pocket knives to name a few.

The paintings of noted illustrators like N.C. Wyeth, Norman Rockwell and Maxfield Parrish are among his traditional influences. Also the films of Walt Disney, George Lucas and Steven Spielberg are sources of inspired imagery.

Clients include Harper/Collins, Penguin, Leisure, Bantam and Doubleday books. Other clients include G.T. Interactive Software, Wizards of the Coast, Milton Bradley, and The Franklin Mint.

Like many illustrators, Matt is influenced by the wonderful work and technological advancements currently taking place in the illustration field. In the last few years he has moved to doing most of his work in 'digital paint'. He must point out, however, the computer is not the "push button" solution many perceive it to be. The same craft and attention to design must be present for the artwork to succeed no matter what the medium.

Matt is also a member of the Society Of Illustrators, New York and the Association for Science Fiction and Fantasy Artists (ASFA). He currently lives in Delaware.

principles of fire

"Tolar!" Zaehr rolled to her feet, her burned lips drawn back across her fangs.

The dragon flung the corpse to the side, a casual gesture that sent the broken body skidding across the cobblestones. It turned toward Zaehr and fixed her with its luminous gaze. Pure, unreasoning terror gripped her—the raw panic a predator instills in its prey.

"Tolar had no place in such a battle," the dragon said. Its voice was thunder and steam, a rumbling hiss that Zaehr felt in her bones. Its crimson scales glittered in the torchlight, as if painted in fresh blood. Black ivory punctuated this ruddy armor—two dark horns stretching back over its massive head and ebon talons longer than any of Zaehr's blades. Even its teeth were dark, as if burned black by the flames that licked around its jaws. But the true fire was in its eyes: The blazing orange orbs consumed her thoughts, reducing her to a frightened child. It took all her strength of will to tear her gaze away, to wrap one hand around the hilt of a curved dagger.

How had it come to this?

"This ends now."

The rumbling voice tore Zaehr back to the present. The knife slid into her hand. Her wounds burned,

by Keith baker

and she fell into a defensive crouch, ready to leap. The dragon towered above her, rearing back on its hind legs, jaws wide. Time slowed to a crawl, and Zaehr could see the light rising in the gullet of the beast.

Fire, she thought. It had begun with fire.

The sky above Sharn was on fire. The shockwave swept across them. A dwarf woman standing nearby was thrown off the edge of the bridge and tumbled howling to the streets below. Dozens of others smashed against the cobblestones, Tolar along with them. Only Zaehr kept her footing; she let the force throw her back and turned the motion into a spinning leap, landing smoothly on her feet. Throughout the twisting roll she kept her eyes on the sky, watching the terrifying spectacle above.

Pride of the Storm was coming apart.

The airship was the largest she had ever seen, the pride of House Lyrandar, a glorious yacht held aloft by twin rings of elemental power. The kraken was on the seal of House Lyrandar, and the ship was designed so that a mighty kraken appeared to be clutching the rear of the boat, four darkwood tentacles stretching out to grip the two massive rings of elemental energy surrounding the vessel.

At least, that was the design.

Zaehr loved airships, and she watched the skies when business brought her and Tolar to the vicinity of Lyrandar Tower. She had been watching when a skycoach rammed into the ship and exploded, leaving a gaping hole in the side of *Pride* and shattering two of the

four supports. The ring of elemental fire collapsed, and a moment later there was a second explosion, greater than the first. Fire flooded the sky, accompanied by a roar that shook the towers and a wave of force that threw Zaehr's companions to the stones. While flame engulfed the ship, the stabilizing ring of elemental air was still holding her aloft—at least for now. But even as Zaehr reached down to help Tolar to his feet, she could see that the ring was losing its integrity. Zaehr knew what would happen next. The ring would collapse, and the burning ship would plummet to the depths of Sharn, smashing against bridges and towers until she finally reached the distant streets. It was inevitable.

The cloudbelt buckled, and the blazing vessel tilted crazily in the sky, charred corpses skidding off the deck and into the air. It was just what Zaehr had seen in her mind.

Except for the dragon.

The ring of air flickered, died, and the ship fell. A new force ripped through the stern, scattering shards of burning wood across the sky. This was no explosion. It was a dragon, a massive creature covered with mirror-bright silver scales—and it was growing. With every second the dragon increased in size and the ship splintered around it.

There was no time to waste.

Zaehr reached deep inside, calling on the natural power within her. Zaehr was a shifter, a blend of human and animal. Many said that the shifters were the thin-blooded children of werewolves, but Tolar swore there was rat and hound in her ancestry. Her senses were sharper than those of any human, and she was swift and strong. When she called upon her animal spirit, her speed became super-human, matching any horse.

She snatched Tolar and lifted him off his feet. The old man was over six feet in height, but he was bone-thin, and the shifter had no trouble carrying him. She charged forward, plowing into people on the bridge as she moved. She heard curses and cries, and a few angry feet and fists lashed at her. People were frightened and confused, and Zaehr knew humans often found her to be an intimidating sight. Her eyes were gleaming red, her skin snow-white, her hair a ghostly silver-white mane, and when she was drawing on her inner spirit as she was now, her mouth was a distended snout filled with razor-sharp teeth. The people were dazed from the ex-plosion, and now this fearsome shifter was ramming into them. But there was no time to explain.

"Get off the bridge!" she snarled. She slammed into a small child, sending him reeling back toward Stonebridge Tower.

A massive chunk of burning wood crashed into the space where she had been standing.

This was followed by a flash of silver—a dragon's tail?—and a thunderous impact that shat-tered the bridge. Chunks of stone joined the cascade of wood, fire, and flesh tumbling to the streets far below. There was a moment of silence. Zaehr had just saved these peoples' lives, but terror and confusion outweighed any sense of gratitude.

"Put me down." Tolar's voice was cool and calm. Zaehr had never seen the old man lose his composure. She set him down, and he walked over to the jagged edge of the bridge and stared down at the path of destruction, thoughtfully running a finger across his red-and-white beard.

Zaehr stepped up beside him. She released her hold on the animal spirit and felt her teeth and jaws retract to their natural shape. Looking down, she could see flames where fragments of the burning hull had lodged along bridges and tower walls. She could see a greater light below, where the ship had finally struck ground.

"Get down there," Tolar said. He'd pro-duced a silver disk from one of his belt pouches, and he pressed it into her hand without looking at her. "The flames will soon consume what the impact left behind. Study the point of collision and any bodies you can find—especially the dragon."

"Right." Zaehr looked at the disk, bright metal embossed with the image of a single feather. A wind token, designed to protect people who fell from towers or bridges by slowing the descent at the last minute. "And you?"

"There are other matters I must attend to," Tolar said. The breeze snapped at his long burgundy overcoat. He looked up at the sky, studying the shattered moorings on Lyrandar tower.

"Right," Zaehr said. "To work, then. And thanks for, you know, saving my life."

Tolar ignored the sarcasm. "Go."

Zaehr sighed. She'd done this before, but it wasn't something you soon grew used to. Taking a deep breath, she wrapped her fingers tightly around the wind token and dived off the edge of the broken bridge. *How did I get into this?* she thought.

It was a rhetorical question. Tolar had found her in the sewers of Sharn. Most likely she'd been born to one of the bands of shifters that lurked in the undercity, surviving by scavenging the midden heaps and sifting through the garbage of the world above. Tolar believed that her family had abandoned her because of the strange color of her skin and eyes, most likely leaving her to die—but she'd proven to be a survivor. Tolar had been an old man even then, facing a young and feral shifter who could only speak a few words. Tolar Velderan was an inquisitive. He made his livelihood

through investigation. He'd never said what task had brought him to the depths that day, but he'd chosen to solve her mystery. He'd calmed her and convinced her to follow him to the surface. In the months and years that followed, he taught her to speak, to read, to follow the pulse of information as it flowed through the streets. She'd saved him a dozen times. But he'd given her life. Without him, Zaehr would still be hunting rats in the dark. He was the only father she'd ever had.

The streets of Sharn rushed up to meet her. She could feel the heat rising from the burning yacht. The magic of the medallion took hold, slowing her descent, and she twisted in the air, adjusting her weight so that she'd drift to the side instead of landing in the wreckage. A crowd had gathered around the shattered ship, and she wondered how many had been crushed beneath her.

The destruction of a Lyrandar airship was a remarkable event. But the dragon? That was something else entirely. A dragon was a thing of legend. It was said that the world itself was formed from a battle between three celestial dragons. The first age of Eberron was a time of terror when fiends and demons ruled the world—until the dragons had risen up and imprisoned these dark spirits in the depths of the underworld. Since then there were stories of the occasional dragon sighting. A drunken explorer once told Zaehr that he'd encountered a dragon with scales the color of midnight in an ancient ruin in the jungles of Q'barra, but he'd also claimed to have found a diamond the size of his head and then dropped it from his airship. Zaehr had always thought that both tales were simply in his imagination.

What lay before her was no adventurer's tale. The silver dragon was tangled in the wreckage of the ship, its head still hidden inside the shattered vessel. It was crumpled and twisted, but Zaehr guessed that it was over eighty feet long from the tip of its muscular tail to the hidden jaws. Its hind legs had been shattered by the impact, and Zaehr noticed that even its blood looked like liquid silver, leaking out from between the armored scales and hissing against the flames. She touched down on the cobblestones next to the dragon's left hind foot. Even its toes were larger than she was.

It's just another victim, Zaehr thought, and it's time to get to work.

A dozen different blades were tucked along the black leather harness Zaehr wore, and she selected one—a thin stiletto she liked to use as a probe. Stepping up to the dragon's foot she fought to shut out the screams and yammering of the surrounding crowd, focusing her attention on the sight of the corpse, and more importantly, on the smell—the world of scent that humans couldn't begin to understand. Fire, blood, wood, heat, and dozens of shattered lives—all of these stories stretched out before her, painted in the language of scent. Strongest of all was the smell of fresh rain—a smell that soon she realized was the odor of the dragon's blood.

Silver rain battled burning wood as Zaehr grew closer to the ship. The vessel was still burning, but Zaehr had no fear of fire. Tolar had told her to trace the corpses, and it was possible there were survivors. Besides, she wanted to see the creature's head. Ignoring the crowd, Zaehr leaped onto the side of the stricken dragon and climbed along its chest, pulling herself to an opening in the hull of the shattered ship.

She'd wanted to see the dragon's head. But the legends, her expectations . . . nothing had prepared her for what she found inside.

The smell of blood and smoke filled Zaehr's nostrils—the coppery tang of human blood blended with the thick rain-scent of the silver dragon. The floor was at a sharp angle, but Zaehr was a talented climber. Her fingernails and toenails were thicker and stronger than those of a human, coming to a natural point, and they helped her maintain a grip on the wooden surface. Absently, she brushed the back of her hand against the steel studs embedded in her black leather jerkin, activating the enchantment held within the armor—a spell that helped to hide her from prying eyes and to disperse any sounds she might make. Zaehr didn't know what she might find in the ship, but she was a hunter by nature—and she'd decide whether or not to reveal herself.

She was standing in a small stateroom. The eastern wall had been shattered by the expanding dragon, but she caught the scent of human blood within the rubble and saw a finger protruding from under a plank.

Carefully sifting through the wood, she found the body of a young male half-elf wearing the bloodstained livery of House Lyrandar—a servant from the look of him, lacking the rough hands of a sailor or the clothing of a House noble. The fire hadn't killed him. From the looks of the corpse, the explosion hadn't reached him. But the damage was terrible. Both his lungs had collapsed, and he had at least a dozen broken bones. Blood was still flowing from his mouth.

As powerful as the explosion had been, much of its force had blasted away from the ship; it might have knocked this boy off his feet, but it hadn't killed him. The dragon had done that. Its body had expanded, smashing through walls and finally through the hull itself, crushing everything in its way in an inexorable tide of armored flesh. Glancing around and tasting the air, Zaehr identified another dozen corpses buried in the rubble. A few carried the scent of burned flesh, no doubt drawn from deeper in the ship and closer to the explosions. The others had been caught in the path of the dragon and crushed like ants beneath a child's foot.

As Tolar had commanded, Zaehr paused to take a quick trace item from each of the corpses she could reach—a scrap of cloth, a lock of hair. She carried a few strips of fresh linen in her pouch; she dabbed one on the silver blood of the dragon and rubbed another against a thick scale.

She pressed forward, working her way deeper into the ruined ship. She could hear voices shouting outside the vessel—officers of the Sharn Watch, a Lyrandar salvage team, healers from House Jorasco. The watch was working to push the public back while the House forces extinguished the fires and brought their own teams into the ship. There wouldn't be much work for the Jorasco healers. Between the impact of the crash, the two explosions, and the crushing bulk of the dragon itself, Zaehr had yet to find anyone who could possibly be revived. During her childhood in the depths and her time with Tolar, Zaehr had seen many horrible things, but finding three young girls crushed against a doorframe . . . what sort of person would set such horror in motion?

She found the center of the first blast—a large dining hall. The walls were covered with ash, and a number of the blackened corpses had been blown apart before being crushed by the dragon. Zaehr found the remnants of a giant owl, most likely a merchant from Dura or a windchasing champion; she plucked a few feathers from one scorched wing. After searching for trace objects on the other corpses, she scoured the room for remnants of the airship that had struck it, then turned her attention to the dragon. Only the muscular neck remained, rammed through the wall leading to the bow of the ship. Zaehr pulled herself along the serpentine neck, squeezing through the smashed gap.

She had a strong stomach. She had spent her first years in filth and had just examined a score of corpses, but what she saw next brought bile to her throat, and it took all her will to keep from retching.

Soon enough the ship was crawling with Lyrandar salvagers, and Zaehr made her way back to the square. She planned to disappear into the shadows, but a skycoach was waiting for her, the steersman carrying a parchment with Tolar's crest. Normally Zaehr loved riding in the air, but after the fall of the *Pride*, she felt a momentary trepidation at stepping aboard the flying boat. But it wasn't in her nature to argue with Tolar. Once she was aboard, the skycoach rose into the air, winding through the massive towers of Sharn and finally bringing Zaehr to the luxurious residential district of Oak Towers. The buildings on this level of Sharn were inspired by elven architecture, with rounded, curving walls and intricate engraving. Most were built from densewood—a form of lumber with the strength and durability of stone.

Tolar was waiting in a small park filled with bloodvines and gray oaks, and Zaehr quickly relayed the highlights of her investigation. Tolar led her down a road cobbled with disks of densewood as they spoke.

"Precisely what I expected," Tolar said when Zaehr told him the story.

"You *expected* the head to be missing?" Climbing along the neck, Zaehr had actually dug one hand into the charred flesh of the beast's stump.

"Missing or at least severely damaged," Tolar said. He was favoring his left leg and placing much of his weight on a gnarled cane. Apparently the morning's excitement had taken its toll, but Zaehr had other concerns.

"Explain," she said. Finding the seared stump of the neck had sent a chill through her. The dragon's head must have been ten feet long. How could something like that simply vanish? She'd half-expected to find some sort of terrible head-eating beast lurking in the wreckage, but she'd seen nothing of the sort.

"When the dragon burst through the hull of the ship, there was no sign of motion in its limbs that could not be explained by the wind and fall. Such an experience would be extremely uncomfortable for the creature in any case. The logical explanation was that the dragon had been concealed on the ship in the form of a smaller creature and that this magical effect was broken upon its death . . . as is typical of such transformations."

"But—" Zaehr knew it was a mistake the moment she opened her mouth. Tolar hated interruptions, and she could sense his frustration in a half-dozen ways—the tightlipped scowl, the lines on his forehead, the sour smell no human would have noticed. She bit her lip even as Tolar silenced her with a sharp wave of his hand.

"I had an excellent view of the creature during those first moments, and there were no signs of mortal injury that I could see—minor burns and scrapes most likely caused by bursting through the hull of the ship. Therefore, the killing blow had to have struck an area of the body that was hidden from view." He paused, glancing back at her for the first time in the conversation. "Now, I believe you had a question?"

"Yes, but . . . the head was *gone*. How does something so large just vanish?"

"You're not thinking on the proper scale," Tolar replied. She could sense his slight disappointment and felt a touch of shame. "When the attack came, the dragon was in the form of another creature—most likely, a human, elf, or half-elf. The injury came while she was in this shape."

Zaehr opened her mouth to speak but bit back the question. One interruption was bad enough.

"I suspect that she was standing close to the breach in the hull during first explosion," Tolar said. "I already mentioned the minor burns. However, her head—barely the size of yours, I imagine—must have been exposed to the full force of the blast. You said the stump of the neck was charred."

Zaehr nodded.

"So the head was blown apart. Most likely pieces remain, but they would have been scattered during the expansion of the rest of the body—I suspect a few curious children will go home with dragon's teeth tonight."

"You said *she.*"

"Yes?" Tolar said.

"You didn't notice?" Zaehr blinked.

"Well, I . . ." She shook her head. "It was a *dragon!* A *myth!* How am I supposed to tell the difference between girls and boys?"

"Dragons are living creatures, Zaehr. And that means that they eat, sleep—and breed."

Zaehr held up her hands. "Until today, I thought dragons were just something cartographers put on maps to justify the regions they were too lazy to explore. I've never considered the idea of where little dragons come from. And you're not the *least* bit surprised to find a dragon in Sharn?"

"Of course not. Sharn is the largest city in Khorvaire—possibly the largest in the modern age. It's a center for trade, diplomacy, and all manner of intrigue. If a dragon is going to move among humanity, do you suppose it would live on a farm? Clearly the creature was here to monitor events in Sharn."

"But why?"

Tolar rubbed his short beard, fingering the streaks of red. "The Library of Korranberg has an excellent draconic studies department. The latest research indicates that while dragons are mortal, they can live for thousands of years. Now look at the last five thousand years of history. Humanity has gone from a state of savagery to dominating two continents. Your race didn't even exist back then. The younger races must move very quickly from the perspective of a dragon. It's hardly surprising that they should wish to study events from within . . . or, I suppose, to control them."

"But . . . if power is what they want, why not just use force? You didn't get as close to that thing as I did, but *I* wouldn't try fighting it if it was alive!"

Tolar stopped walking. He turned to her and put a hand on her shoulder, staring down into her eyes. Whenever he looked at her that way, Zaehr always remembered their first meeting in the sewers so many years ago—that absolute confidence that had caused her to hold her attack, the determination that had drawn her up into the civilized world.

"Look beyond the obvious, child. If the tales are true, the civilization of the dragons is over a hundred thousand years old. These creatures . . . they are the children of Eberron and Siberys, the earth and sky. Magic is in their blood. Now look at us, with our short lives and the narrow-mindedness that accompanies such frailty. Weak but arrogant, always pressing forward, shattering walls and breaking barriers, heedless of what might be on the other side. The great Houses always striving for more gold. The nations going to war for pride and ambition—and these last few years

have shown us the price of such arrogance."

He was referring to the Mourning, the disaster that had destroyed the nation of Cyre and brought an end to the Last War . . . at least for now. No one knew the cause of the Mourning, but most assumed it was tied to the war—either a new weapon that spun out of control or the combined result of the magical forces used during the war.

"What would the dragons have to gain from conquering us?" Tolar continued. "Even if they had the power, why would they want such short-sighted subjects?"

"To keep things like the Mourning from happening again."

Tolar nodded, and Zaehr could sense his satisfaction in the minute shift of his mouth and the faintest change to his scent. "A good answer. But perhaps they wish to help us find that path for ourselves instead of forcing us on it. Where are the gods?"

"What?"

"The gods. The Sovereign Host. People revere them, believe that they guide and protect, but you never *see* them. If the gods exist, why wouldn't they conquer the world to enforce proper behavior?"

"That's why I've never believed in gods," Zaehr said.

Tolar smiled. "Ah, yes. The eternal pragmatist." He dismissed the conversation with a wave of his hand and began walking again. "We're wasting time. Tell me what else you found. I want to know everything before we arrive at Stormwind Keep."

"Stormwind Keep?"

"Home to Lord Dantian d'Lyrandar, the owner of *Pride of the Storm.*" He smiled ever so slightly and tapped his cane against the densewood cobble. "It seems we have a mystery to solve."

"Here's a mystery," Zaehr said. "Why do people *build* things like this?"

Dantian d'Lyrandar was a dragonmarked lord of the House of Storm, heir to the Lyrandar line's mystical power to control wind and water. House Lyrandar had built a vast mercantile empire around this magical ability. Their raincallers provided "insurance" against drought to the farmers of Galifar, a policy some called extortion. Lyrandar merchantmen had long dominated the seas, and now their airships were carving new trade routes across the sky. Only half-elves could carry the mark, and for many people Lyrandar defined the race. Certainly it had transformed them from a race of outcasts to a proud folk who stood on equal ground with both humans and elves.

Dantian's abode spoke to that pride. A densewood funnel stained in black and silver, shaped like a tornado rising up to the sky, formed the base of the tower. This was topped by a massive kraken, whose long tentacles wrapped around the tower. The beast was carved from densewood, but it was remarkably realistic; the blue paint covering its skin glistened as if wet. The eyes of the kraken were octagonal windows, and golden light burned behind the panes.

"The kraken is the sigil of House Lyrandar," Tolar said.

"He's got his kraken boat and his kraken house. Does he wear a big golden kraken with tentacles wrapped around his chin?"

"It is his gold, Zaehr, to dispose of as he will."

Zaehr growled. Her childhood had been a constant struggle for survival, and she still felt an instinctive disdain for the wealthy.

"Where's the door?" she said as they drew closer to the tower. While a broad stairway rose up from the street, it came to a stop at the junction of two tentacles.

"I'm sure it will appear, in due time," Tolar said. He paused at the base of the steps. "What can you tell me?"

Zaehr studied the labyrinth of sounds and smells around her. Following scents was like gazing into the past, and city streets were always overwhelmingly chaotic, flowing with the traces of hundreds of people. It was as difficult to pluck a scent from this mass as it would be to listen to a whispered conversation in a noisy crowd, yet the task had its own satisfaction, much like piecing together a complex puzzle.

"A gargoyle has been here within the last hour," she said, closing her eyes to better taste the wind. "Been and gone, staying only for a few moments. A gnome came later—ink and leather, still within. Many half-elves. Perfume and silk in the past, but the recent smells are soot and rain." She breathed in again. "Unless it rained in the last hour and I didn't notice, I think it's the blood of the dragon."

"As expected," Tolar said. "You said Lyrandar salvagers were at the scene. Naturally one or more would arrive to inform Lord Dantian of the disaster." He started up the flight of stairs and was halfway up when a voice rang out.

"Who approaches?" It was deep and inhuman, the sound of a storm at sea.

"Tolar Velderan, from the Globe Agency of House Tharashk," Tolar replied. "And my associate Zaehr. We are expected."

"You were not called for."

"Nonetheless, we *are* expected. Lord Dantian received a message from Lady Solia d'Lyrandar within the last hour, delivered by gargoyle courier. Surely Lord Dantian will respect his aunt's wishes on the matter."

No response. The only sound was the faint wind blowing through the densewood spires.

"We're working for Globe?" Zaehr whispered. "How did *that* happen?" The dragonmarked House Tharashk used its Mark of Finding to dominate the field of private investigation. Tolar was bound to the house by blood, but he did not bear the dragonmark, and there was a rift between the old man and a few of his more successful relatives—especially Lady Kava of the Globe.

"I still have connections in the house, child," Tolar murmured. "And it's not every day we see something like this. Now hush."

A moment later, the wooden tentacles before them burst into animate life, pulling back to reveal a massive doorway. The door split down the center and creaked inwards.

"Enter."

Zaehr stepped in front of Tolar. She did not draw any of her knives, but her hands were poised by her favorite blades, and every muscle was tensed and ready for action. Cautiously, she stepped into the hall.

Fresh rain.

The smell of mist and water filled the hall—the scent she had judged to be the blood of the dragon outside. It overpowered all lesser odors and had to be generated by magic. But to what end? Did Dantian d'Lyrandar enjoy the smell of the storm, or was there some stench he wished to conceal?

"Welcome to Stormwind Keep!" a voice boomed.

As a race, half-elves were not known for their girth. Whether it was cultural or the result of their fey heritage, the half-elves were usually slender and delicate. The speaker shattered these expectations. Zaehr and Tolar could have both fit beneath the man's silk robes and had room to spare.

"I am Kestal Haladan, and it is my honor to manage Lord Dantian's affairs." His eyes twinkled beneath deep rolls of flesh. He mopped his brow with a heavily scented kerchief, and Zaehr wrinkled her nose at the sweet smell. "You, good man?" he said to Tolar, "You are the representative of the Globe Agency? My humblest apologies for the delay at the gate. We were of the impression that our inquisitive would have a little more . . . gray blood in his veins."

"Gray" was a polite way of saying "orcish." House Tharashk had emerged from the mingling of human refugees with orcs in the western swamps known as the Shadow Marches. Most people associated House Tharashk with orcs and half-orcs, but there were just as many humans in the house as orcs.

"I assure you, we are quite capable of handling the task at hand," Tolar said.

"No." A new voice rang through the hall. A man, young and arrogant. *"We can handle this task. Your services will not be required."*

"Lord Dantian!" Kestal Haladan made a surprisingly graceful bow considering his girth. "My lord, I was going to bring your guests to the lower hall. . . ."

"No." Lord Dantian d'Lyrandar was dressed for battle. Four silver lightning bolts adorned a jerkin of oiled leather, and a dark blue cloak flowed across his shoulders. His pale white hair was held back by a narrow circlet of gold, adorned with a writhing kraken.

His right hand clenched the gilded hilt of a fine longsword. "I have no intention of granting my hospitality to these . . . people."

"Lord Lyrandar," Tolar replied, "it is not your decision to make."

Zaehr stepped between the two men before Dantian's blade was fully drawn. She caught the half-elf's wrist and showed him her teeth. "Don't," she said, and she could see her blood-red eyes reflected in his furious gaze.

"Guards!" cried Haladan.

Zaehr could feel Dantian's surging emotions in the tension of his wrist, the flicker of his eyes, the shifting scent that rose over the smell of rain. "We were sent for," she whispered, tightening her grip until he released his sword. "We just want to talk, but if you start a fight . . ." As Zaehr spoke, her jaws extended, fangs stretching down in a vicious wolf-like snout. "I'll rip your face off."

A half-dozen guards had responded to the alarm, and they surrounded Zaehr and Dantian, iron-shod clubs at the ready. Zaehr knew that if she harmed the Lyrandar lord, it probably would be the last thing she did, but she kept her gaze on his, holding the promise of bloodshed in her eyes.

"Well?" she said.

She knew his answer before he spoke, and she let go of his hand even as he opened his mouth.

"Fine," he said, taking a step back. "I suppose I should indulge Aunt Solia. Haladan, I'll receive them in the garden." He turned and walked down the hall, gingerly rubbing his right wrist.

"Very well, my lord." The servant scowled at Zaehr, his beady eyes dark points in his flabby face. "If you'll follow me. . . ."

⸺✦⸺

Lord Dantian proved as good as his word. He might have set the guards upon Zaehr the moment he was safely out of reach of her fangs. Although he sought no vengeance for the blow to his pride, Dantian was no fool. A squad of guards remained with Zaehr and Tolar as they traveled deeper into the keep, and these soldiers watched Zaehr's every movement.

Dantian's garden was another toy, a chance for the young lord to show off his wealth and power. The circular chamber lay at the center of the tower, but for all appearances it was an open-air park, the ceiling masked by cunning illusion. A paved path wove between dark grass, well-groomed trees, and displays of exotic wildflowers.

It was raining.

Rain in Sharn was a common occurrence. Tolar's long coat was oiled cloth, and he drew his hood up over his face. Zaehr liked the rain. She had spent her first years around water, and while it was hard to be truly nostalgic for a life in the sewers, she had never minded getting wet.

Still, she guessed that the rain wasn't intended as a gift, and this seemed to be confirmed when the drizzle faded away just before Lord Dantian returned. The illusory clouds evaporated, leaving blue sky and bright sun—though it did not escape Zaehr's notice that the sunlight provided no heat.

"I apologize for my brusque behavior." Dantian had changed his clothes and was wearing blue and black robes in place of his armor. "Baroness Solia has instructed that I assist you within reason, and it is not my place to question my aunt."

"Don't you *want* to know who destroyed your ship?" Zaehr said.

"I *do* know." He jabbed a slender finger at Tolar. "You. Your kind."

"Old men?" Zaehr said. She could still sense Dantian's rage. It didn't seem to be an act.

Tolar said nothing.

"Tharashk!" Dantian roared. "You foul graybloods with your druids and your dragons!"

Zaehr glanced at Tolar, nonplussed.

"I assure you, Lord Dantian, we have no idea what you are talking about," Tolar said. "My own ties to the House are—"

"Don't try to deny it. I know all about your kind. And *yours.*" A glare at Zaehr. "Do you think this is the first airship we've lost? I've done my research. Wretched druids, trying to stop progress. *Druids.* And who were the first druids? *Orcs.* And *shifters.* And who taught the first druids? *Dragons.* It all comes together, doesn't it? You're *still* working with these hidden dragons. You destroy our ships. And who gets called in to investigate? *You* do. At least this time your damned dragon was caught in the blast."

"Lord Dantian," Tolar said, "while your theories are most intriguing, I have my own paths of inquiry I should like to pursue. And Lady Solia has ordered you to—"

"I know what my aunt requires," Dantian growled. "Just as I know she's wasting her time. And mine. So what is it you want?"

"A list of all those aboard *Pride of the Storm* at the time of the explosion, making note of those who lived and died. As I was unaware of any similar incidents, I should like a list of those as well, along with any organizations or individuals you might have quarreled with recently."

Dantian glared at Tolar but said nothing.

"I will also need to speak with the surviving elemental heart of the *Pride.*"

This meant nothing to Zaehr, but it certainly produced a violent reaction from Dantian. "How do you know about that?" he said, clenching his fists. The wind rose, and Zaehr guessed that the brewing storm might be the accidental child of the Lyrandar lord's fury.

"Anyone can study the most basic principles of elemental binding, Lord Dantian," Tolar said. "And the second explosion aboard *Pride of the Storm* was the result of the detonation of the fire heart. There was no similar release of air. Therefore the elemental that empowered the ring of air is still contained. I'm sure such an artifact would be the first thing your salvage teams would recover, and I imagine you'd get a gnome translator to come and transcribe the spirit's memories of the events. Perhaps the gnome who arrived just before we did? While I'm sure the report will be most informative, I wish to speak to the elemental myself."

Dantian's fury had given way to sheer surprise. For a moment he stood in silence. Finally, he grimaced and gave a curt nod.

"And the other information?" Tolar asked.

Dantian glanced at the portly servant. "Haladan will take care of it for you." He looked back at Tolar. His gaze was hard. "I warn you, grayblood, my aunt will hear of this, and now. If *anything* happens to the heart, I'll put you and your dog in the ground."

"Of course," Tolar said, unmoved. "Now, if you can show us the way? There's work to be done."

Lord Dantian took his leave. Another six guards took his place, and Zaehr could smell their hostility. Clearly Dantian was prepared to make good on his threat. Zaehr hoped that the old man knew what he was doing with this elemental heart.

"So *did* your family have anything to do with it?" she whispered to Tolar, as they made their way up a spiral staircase.

He said nothing, but the disappointment in his expression was answer enough.

"Just asking," she said, keeping her voice low and an eye on the nearest guard. "We've had troubles with your cousins in the past. If there's something I need to know—"

He cut her off with a curt shake of the head. "Lord Dantian's delusions are just that. There are no ties between my family and the druids of the west, especially the more violent sects.

Though it is curious that he has formed a link in his mind between dragons and druids."

"They don't mix?"

"Not now. It's said that it was a dragon who first brought the secrets of natural magic to the orcs, who later shared it with humanity. But that was thousands of years ago—and a legend at that, not a tale I'd expect a rather spoiled Lyrandar lord to have heard."

"So you're *not* planning on destroying this magic heart?"

His eyes widened in fractional surprise. "Even if I possessed the means to do such a thing, why would I?"

Zaehr shrugged. "You say that as if you've never sprung a surprise on me before. If it does come to a fight, I think I can bring down six of these sentries, but I'm leaving the rest to you."

"Then I suppose I'll have to be on my best behavior," he said, with a faint smile. "But I must say I'm disappointed. A year ago I would have expected eight. Are you finally learning restraint?"

Zaehr grinned. "Ask again tomorrow," she said.

Kestal Haladan led them to a small chamber high in the tower. Zaehr stepped in first to examine the room. The western wall was dominated by a massive octagonal window, and she realized that this was one of the eyes of the sculpted kraken atop the tower. This room was a sharp contrast to the luxurious appointments they had seen so far. The walls and floor were completely bare, and there were only three pieces of furniture in the room: a sturdy densewood table and two stone pedestals. One of these pedestals was currently empty. The other held a steel sphere roughly the same size as a human head. Drawing closer, Zaehr saw that it was actually a complex metal latticework laid atop a large chunk of crystal. The table was empty, but the scents told a tale. Two half-elves wearing leather and steel had brought the sphere into the chamber within the last two hours. A gnome had followed—male, young, accompanied by scents of ink and paper. He'd sat on the table, no doubt scribbling notes. Moments ago, one of the original guards had returned and approached the gnome, and the two had left together.

Zaehr turned to explain this to Tolar, but he stepped across the threshold and into the room.

The wind howled.

It was a mighty gale . . . or so it seemed. The sound was that of a hurricane wailing through a canyon, a storm that could flay flesh from bone.

But there was no wind. Just sound.

Zaehr and the guards had drawn their weapons, but Tolar was as calm as ever. He opened his mouth and produced an astonishing noise—a loud hissing and spitting not unlike the sound of the storm itself. The wailing dropped in volume. Tolar continued his choking diatribe, and soon the storm faded completely.

Zaehr and the guards stared.

"Auran," the old man said. "Difficult on the throat and agony to learn but rewarding in its way."

Zaehr glanced around the room, sliding her daggers back into their sheaths. "That was a *conversation?*"

"Of course." Tolar gestured at the sphere of crystal and steel. "Normally the spirit is dormant, barely aware of its surroundings. But between the recent disaster and being separated from its ship, it's frustrated and awake."

"What's it got against you?"

"Nothing. I suspect it was just the number of people in the room at once that disturbed it. It doesn't perceive the world in the same way that we do, and it doesn't understand our reality. As far as it's concerned, we are small masses of water. It's uncomfortable around any element except air." He turned to look at Haladan. "I need those lists your lord promised me, as quickly as possible."

Haladan frowned but gave a short bow. "I'll see to it. Captain . . ." He glanced at the commander of the guards, a half-elf woman who might have been beautiful if not for a ghastly scar gouged down the left side of her face. "You heard Lord Dantian. If our guests do anything to threaten you or the heart . . . act decisively."

The woman smiled. Half of her smile was a wall of gold. She'd lost a few teeth when she bought her scar. Zaehr smiled back, drawing her own lips away from her long canine fangs.

As Haladan turned to go, Zaehr caught the faintest trace of a familiar scent. "Were you onboard the *Pride* today?" she asked.

Haladan shook his head. "Not at all," he said, mopping his brow with perfumed silk. "I'm embarrassed to say I am quite afraid of heights. I stay indoors whenever possible. Why do you ask?"

"It's not important," Zaehr said. Surely it was the scent of rain, confusing her senses.

Tolar had already turned his attention back to the crystal orb, and now he spoke again in the strange language of the winds. The sphere howled in response, and Zaehr saw faint arcs of lightning crackling around the steel cage.

The conversation continued for a few minutes before Zaehr's patience wore thin. "What is it saying?" she asked.

Tolar was annoyed, as she'd expected, but he indulged her curiosity. "It's frustrated. It doesn't understand the nature of the binding, but it hates not being in the air. When it was part of the ship, it was still in motion and that kept it content. I'm trying to learn about the people on the ship, but as I expected it simply thinks the ship was full of water."

He proceeded with a new series of rasps and wheezes, and the caged wind responded with moans. "Ah!" he said with a note of triumph. But instead of explaining, he launched into another throat-rending exchange, brushing aside Zaehr's inquiries. Finally, both Tolar and the sphere fell silent. The old man blinked and rubbed his throat. "Could I get a goblet of water, fair lady?" he said to the guard. "And you can inform Master Haladan that our business here is done."

"So?"

They were back on the streets of Oak Towers. It had taken a little longer for Haladan to provide Tolar with the information the old man had required, but they had eventually made their way out of Stormwind Keep and back into the sunlit streets of upper Sharn. Tolar had refused to discuss his conversation with the elemental while they were in the building, but Zaehr wasn't about to give up now.

"So . . . ?" Tolar echoed.

"What did it say? I know that 'ah.' That was a 'just as I expected' ah."

Tolar smiled. "I suppose it was. I told you it thought the ship was full of water. But there were a few exceptions. It could sense the presence of the other elemental—the ring of

fire. It told me that there was an 'older fire' that frequently came and went and that it was this older fire that destroyed the ring of flame . . . that *ordered* it to explode, apparently. The skycoach that crashed into the *Pride* held 'sparks'—most likely some sort of lesser fire elemental."

"But the dragon?"

Tolar stroked his beard. "Dragons have strong elemental ties themselves. They were among the first creatures born on this world, and they are creatures of primal energy—magic and nature, fire and water. The elemental said that it felt a powerful wind close by . . . *before* the skycoach struck."

"So the dragon didn't destroy the ship?"

"Quite the opposite," Tolar said. "I suspect the ship was destroyed because of the dragon. Elementals have little sense of time, but the 'powerful wind' was new on the ship, unlike the water and the 'old fire.' So I suspect it was a guest. Someone who had recently arrived."

"That's still not much to work with," Zaehr said. She'd been studying the scroll Haladan had given them, the list of those on *Pride* at the time of the fall. "There were over a dozen guests onboard."

"Which is why I went to the trouble to obtain this." Tolar produced a second roll of parchment from one deep pocket. Zaehr could see the Lyrandar seal, but there was no trace of the rain-smell of Stormwind Keep. "When I spoke with Lady Solia, I asked *her* for a list of passengers. Compare the two, if you will. I suspect you'll find Lord Lyrandar's list comes up short."

Zaehr unrolled both scrolls and set them down on the pavement, quickly checking names. "You think Dantian lied? Why?"

"Dantian's motives—if they are indeed his—are not yet clear. But if this ship was destroyed because of the dragon, identifying her is the first step in finding the answer."

"Adaila Lantain," Zaehr said. "Both lists are identical except for that one name. A visitor from Morgrave University."

"Good. If she lived in Sharn, we should be able to find more at her abode."

"And now I suppose you expect me to track her down."

Tolar spread his hands. "If it's too much bother, Zaehr, we can always hire an inquisitive."

Zaehr slipped through the crowded streets of the University district. Dusk was falling, and the streets were full of laughing students and somber scholars discussing the lessons of the day, drowning academic concerns in wine and song. Zaehr barely noticed the antics of the revelers. She was on the hunt, and every sense was focused on her prey.

The search had begun in Morgrave University, where a handful of coins had established the path and a picture of her prey. Adaila was a respected historian and attended all gatherings of the sages, but she rarely taught and did not maintain an office at the university. Aside from lectures concerning history and expeditions others intended to make into Xen'drik,

Adaila was almost a hermit. But a favored student recalled seeing her at the Kavallah Concert Hall the previous night, and it was there that Zaehr caught the faintest trace of her in the air—rain and sweet mist, the same odor Zaehr had wiped off the scale. It was marred and masked by the smells of brocade and human flesh, but Zaehr was confident nonetheless.

Is this the smell of the dragon's sweat? Zaehr wondered as she pressed down the streets.

For Zaehr, there was no greater thrill than the urban hunt, tracing a path through the past. Her only regret was that her prey was already dead, denying any chance of a battle at the end of the trail.

The path led back to a book bindery, where Adaila had left three manuscripts for binding—copies of a treatise about the various myths of the legendary conflict between dragons and demons at the dawn of creation. The lady had left her address with the proprietor, and he was willing to exchange the address for three pieces of silver.

Silver coins, silver blood, Zaehr thought. The man clearly had no concept of his client's true nature. Why should he? Who would have thought a mythical creature would try to have a book published by the university?

She was writing a book of myths. Was she writing what she knew to be true or spreading lies to cover the trail? All Zaehr knew of dragons came from legend. If those stories were shaped by the dragons themselves, what could be trusted?

It was a thorny path to walk, but at the end of the day Zaehr was a hunter, not a philosopher. She had found the home of her prey. If there were answers to be found, Tolar would surely dredge them from the dragon's lair. Spotting a stonebeak thrush, Zaehr rubbed the medallion she wore around her neck, whistling an undulating tune. The amulet was a gift from Tolar, and it allowed Zaehr to compel the assistance of small creatures. A moment later the thrush fluttered down and landed on her wrist. Zaehr bound a scrap of parchment to the bird's leg. She whispered to it, impressing the image of the home she shared with Tolar in its mind. A moment later the thrush took to the air, carrying the message down the towers toward her partner.

Even without the bookbinder's help, it would have been a simple matter for Zaehr to find the dragon's lair. By now she had latched onto the human scent that accompanied that faint smell of spring, the odor that had to belong to Adaila's human disguise. As Zaehr followed the scent into the nearby residential district, it began to join up with other trails—faint and ghostly images of Adaila's movements over the past day. All of them came to an end at the door of a small, unpretentious apartment. The door was locked, and Zaehr could smell no other scents leading up to it. Adaila was apparently just as reclusive as reports claimed. There was no garden, and the shades were drawn across the windows. Zaehr ran one sharp fingernail across the lock. Part of her yearned to open the door. The hunt wasn't finished, and there were still mysteries to solve. But her impatience had caused enough problems in the past, and Tolar's instructions were clear: She should wait for him to arrive. Running a hand across the studs on her armor to activate the concealing charm, she slipped into the shadows of a nearby alley and dropped into a comfortable crouch, keeping her eyes on the dragon's door.

It was instinct that had caused her to hide, and instinct served her well. Only minutes passed before three people approached Adaila's home. They were squat, muscular folk shrouded in dark hooded cloaks. They wore black scarves under the hoods, concealing their features. One carried a short spear that seemed to be made from a single piece of brass. The others kept their hands hidden beneath their cloaks, but the bulges spoke of weapons hidden below. At first Zaehr took them for dwarves, but then the wind carried their scent to her hiding place, causing her to wrinkle her nose in surprise.

Fire.

The scent was hot and acrid, the sharp smells of ash and molten metal. These were no dwarves.

The leader reached out and touched the lock. Night had fallen, and there was a flash of light that dispelled the gathering gloom—a spell, or was it simply the creature's skin? Whatever the answer, the lock gave way and the door opened. The three strangers disappeared inside.

Zaehr only waited a moment before following. The ashen stench was familiar—she'd smelled it in the dining hall of *Pride of the*

Storm, though at the time it didn't occur to her that it could be tied to a living creature. *Tolar be damned,* she thought. *If these things are involved in this, they can tell me what's going on.*

Reaching the doorway, Zaehr saw that the lock had been burned away. A small round hole surrounded by charred wood was all that was left. She drew her two favorite blades—heavy knives of orc design, each sharpened on the inner edge of the curved blade. Folding the knives back against her forearms, she slipped silently through the doorway.

The first thing she smelled was smoke, and her ears quickly confirmed it—a fire was growing in the depths of the house. Whatever the creatures were, they had wasted no time. Zaehr moved cautiously down the hall, and in the next room she saw it.

One of the creatures had thrown aside its black cloak. Though it had the muscular build of a dwarf, it was like no dwarf she had ever seen. Its skin was the brilliant orange of a hot coal, and flames licked around its chin in a bizarre parody of a beard. Its eyes were points of blazing light, but they looked right past her. Between her skill and the enchantment woven into her armor, she was still shielded by the shadows. The carpet beneath the creature's feet was burning, and when he turned and laid a hand on a richly upholstered couch, it burst into flames.

Zaehr wanted to know what these creatures were and what their connection was to the *Pride*—but she needed to even the odds before she could start a conversation. She slid up behind the stocky figure, her stealthy motion further masked by the sound of the fire. As the creature reached for a desk covered with papers, she struck, slamming the steel pommels of her blades into the back of her enemy's head. The man staggered, howling in a strange inhuman tongue, filled with pops and hisses. Zaehr had to grit her teeth to keep from crying out herself. The creature's skin was *hot,* searing her skin where she'd brushed against him. Hardly unexpected—but this was not a foe she'd plan to bite.

The sound was sure to summon the creature's companions, and time was of the essence. He turned toward her, a long brass knife in his hands, and made a wild thrust in her direction. Zaehr easily avoided the blow, but the intent was clear—Zaehr might have struck with the pommel, but he was using the blade.

So be it, she thought.

She swept the burning man's blade to the side with one sharp blow, following up with a gash on his wrist. Dark blood pooled along the wound, steaming in the warm air. Before her enemy could recover, she lashed out with twin arcs of deadly steel, digging deeply into both sides of his neck. If he'd been human, the blow would have decapitated him. As it was, he fell to the burning carpet without a sound. Steaming blood poured out of the wounds. An instant later, his body simply dissolved into ash.

With her opponent down, Zaehr studied the room. It was too late to stop the fire—the flames were already spreading to bookshelves and the timbers of the floor, and the smoke was stinging her eyes and burning her throat. She glanced around, trying to see *something* that stood out, something that might be worth this destruction.

The fire was almost her undoing. Her keen senses were dulled by the smoke and the crackling flames, and she almost didn't hear the creature approaching from behind. The flash of motion in her peripheral vision, the heat from the burning spear—she recognized the danger just in time to fling herself forward, rolling and spinning to face her foes. The two remaining fire-folk were there: the squat man with his brass spear and a heavyset woman, the one who had melted the lock with her touch.

Zaehr let fury and instinct take over. Adrenaline surged through her as she flung both knives at the spearman. The first caught him directly in the forehead, cracking the skull and lodging in whatever lay beneath. The second sunk deep in his throat. He let go of his spear, dropped to his knees, and clutched at the handle of the lower knife. Even as he pried it out, his body disintegrated into ash and embers.

Zaehr already had another pair of knives in her hands. "Out on the street!" she snarled at the burning woman, squinting against the smoke. There was no saving the house, but Tolar knew the art of truthtelling, and he could force the stranger to tell them everything.

The glowing creature said nothing. She smiled.

"Don't you understand?" Zaehr said. She raised her knives. "Out now or you join your friends!"

"*You join us all,*" the woman said, in a voice like a roaring bonfire. "*We serve the first fire, and we will return.*"

Zaehr leaped, both knives raised, but she wasn't fast enough.

The woman exploded in a brilliant burst of fire. The shockwave slammed into Zaehr and flung her into a burning bookshelf. Fire swallowed the world.

⚜

"You're lucky to be alive."

Recognition of Tolar's voice—the realization that she *was* alive—was drowned out by the agony that had been dulled by unconsciousness. Each breath brought a wave of pain, the air tearing at her burned lungs.

"Drink."

She didn't want to open her mouth, but the first drop of thick fluid brought a wonderful cooling sensation. She could feel it healing her blackened tongue. She let the potion flow down her throat. The pain slowly receded, and she felt her strength returning.

Zaehr opened her eyes.

She was lying on hard stone. She could see the burns fading from her snow-white skin as the healing potion worked its magic, but she was covered with ash. The smell of smoke clung to her clothes and made it difficult to tell what other scents were in the air, but she saw a black column of smoke rising to the east.

"Is that—?" Her throat was still parched, and her voice cracked.

"Yes," Tolar said. He was sitting on the ground next to her, sifting through a leather satchel. He produced a skin of water and held it to Zaehr's lips. "The building was beyond salvation."

"So she's talking now, is she?" The voice was cold and hard, for all its high timbre. The speaker was barely three feet tall, and Zaehr had the immediate sense that he enjoyed being able to look down at someone. Despite his size, he was no child. He was a gnome, with sharp features and a carefully waxed black beard. "I do so look forward to hearing her explanation."

"If your guards had responded more swiftly, you might have caught the arsonists and saved the building, lieutenant." Tolar said.

Zaehr squinted at the gnome, taking in his green-and-black uniform and the presence of a few larger members of the Sharn Watch standing nearby.

"Yes, well. At least we've done one of those things, yes?"

"You caught them?" Zaehr said. Her thoughts were still thick and muddled, her head filled with wet sand.

"Well, *that's* original," the gnome said. "I suppose you had nothing to do with this? You happened to break in and were prowling around the professor's house when a passing wizard flung a fireball through an open window?"

"Lieutenant," Tolar said quietly, "both my associate and myself are professional inquisitives, fully bonded by House Tharashk. I sent her here in pursuit of an investigation. If you wish, I can establish a truthtelling zone to prove her innocence in this matter."

"Or you'll *say* you're truthtelling," the gnome said with a sneer, "and let her lie to her heart's content."

"Of course not. I'll establish a zone of veracity, which forces all those within its bounds to speak the truth. If you stand next to her, we can easily prove the power of the spell with a few questions about your recent income and commitment to the cause of justice. But perhaps there are more pleasant ways to test the truth of that." He produced a small pouch, which clinked as he flexed his fingers.

The gnome smiled. "When you put it that way . . ." He took the pouch and glanced inside. "Far be it from me to interfere with the work of House Tharashk, though the fire wardens may make their own investigation."

"If they don't trouble us, you'll have as much again at the end of the week."

The lieutenant nodded. "Good luck with your work then. Always a pleasure." He inclined his head and turned away, rejoining the troops who were examining the burned out building.

"I hope we're getting well paid for this job," Zaehr grumbled.

Tolar helped her to her feet. "Well enough," he replied. "I trust you *didn't* burn down the building this time?"

"You'll never let me forget that, will you?" Zaehr said, scowling. "No, this one wasn't me. I think it was the same people who attacked the *Pride.*"

"And they escaped?" Tolar said. "The damage was quite extensive by the time I reached you, but I saw no other bodies."

Zaehr forced herself to sit up. "They just . . . disintegrated. The one who exploded said, 'We will return again.' "

Tolar frowned. "Tell me everything. Quickly."

Zaehr recounted the tale as best as she could. Tolar interrupted with questions.

"When the man dissolved, what happened to his robe and weapons?"

"When you struck him, did the heat of his body damage your blade?"

At last he was satisfied.

"Azers," he said. "Lesser denizens of Fernia, the plane of fire. The 'sparks' the heart mentioned, I am certain. But they could not come here on their own. Some greater power is drawing them to this world."

"The woman said they served the 'first flame.' "

Zaehr knew Tolar as well as anyone. She could read his emotions as easily as a book . . . easier, since she'd never cared much for reading. He tried to conceal his emotions, and a stranger might not have noticed the change, but to Zaehr his surprise and fear were as clear as the peal of the bell that rang the hours.

"What?" she said. "What does it mean?"

"This is no time for discussion," he said, eyes hard. "Did they leave a trail you can follow?"

Zaehr tasted the air. The lingering stench of smoke made it difficult, but the path was there—the threefold trail of molten metal muffled under cloth. Traveling away from the dragon's door and disappearing down and alley.

"Yes," she said, brushing the soot off her clothes and looking back at the ruined cottage. "But first, I need my knives."

Zaehr expected the trail to lead them across the city, to a dark hole in the lower wards where such creatures might hide from common scrutiny. The truth was a disappointment. The alley was a labyrinth that wound behind spires and cottages, but they'd traveled less than a thousand feet when the trail came to end.

"Nothing," she said, studying the surroundings. They were at a juncture of three paths with high walls all around. "It's strong and recent, but it stops dead here." She studied the ground. "It's not just the scent. The physical trail stops too. Could they have teleported?"

"Close," Tolar replied, glancing around. "I suspect they were summoned here, pulled through the planar barriers that separate this world from the endless fires of Fernia. He would have done the same thing when he attacked the *Pride*—prepared the skycoach, summoned the azers to fly it, somehow prepared the fire elemental within the heart to explode when the attack came. There's no sinister headquarters to be found. These henchman appear when needed and vanish the moment the task is done."

"But who?"

"Someone familiar with House Lyrandar. Someone who knew when Adaila Lantain would be onboard and when she would be speaking in the lower hall. Search the area again. If few people have been through here . . . surely our culprit has left a clue."

Zaehr studied the surroundings, reaching out with her senses. She'd been so focused on the burning scent of the azers that she'd completely ignored the other smells and colors of the alley. Rot and mold, the trails of a dozen rats, the usual scents of the city. But one thing stood out—an overwhelming burst in the barren landscape.

Bending down, she lifted a square of muddy silk off the ground with one long fingernail. It still reeked of perfume and the familiar scent of rain.

"House Lyrandar it is," she said.

Tolar nodded. "Yes. It would be. Go back to our office. I'll meet you there in an hour."

"No, you won't." The fear was still there, clouding his countenance. Tolar had often kept secrets from her, but she'd rarely seen him afraid. "What is this?"

"This is no time for discussion," he said, heading toward the main streets. "You will do as I say. You're lucky to be alive, and you will go back to the office and rest. I'll join you soon."

They emerged on a major thoroughfare. Two skycoaches were hovering over the mooring platform. Tolar helped Zaehr into one and placed two silver coins in the hand of the coachman.

"Take her to Dragon Towers," he said.

The coach rose off the platform and began to dip down toward the middle wards. But Zaehr had already produced another silver sovereign, which she flashed before the coachman's eyes. "I've got a better idea," she said, watching as Tolar climbed aboard the other coach and sailed off to the north. "Follow that coach."

⁂

It came as no surprise when Tolar returned to Stormwind Keep. Night had fallen, and the streets were almost empty. Zaehr clung to the shadows as she kept pace with the old man. She didn't know how she'd get past the kraken doors, but in the end it wasn't an issue. The wooden tentacles slid aside the moment Tolar approached with no challenge from the guardian. Once the old man was inside, the tendrils began to descend. Zaehr sprinted forward, and her burst of speed carried her under the massive wooden arms before the portal closed.

Slipping through the gates, she nearly ran into Tolar. The hall was dark, and the old man had paused in the antechamber. He was kneeling over something—a body, stretched out along the floor. The sentry who had been guarding the door when they arrived before.

"Zaehr," he said quietly. "I believe I made my wishes clear."

The gates closed with a solid *thud.* Zaehr and Tolar might have been allowed in, but it appeared that leaving would be a greater challenge.

Zaehr shrugged. "I'm wild and unpredictable. It's endearing."

Tolar sighed, and she could feel his regret.

"What is it?" she said. "And what happened to him?" She nodded at the guard on the ground. She couldn't see any sign of blood, burns, or bruises, but even in the dim light she could see that he was dead.

"Magic," Tolar said. "We're dealing with something ancient and powerful, and I fear it may have anticipated our arrival. But it has already expended a great deal of power today—if we are lucky, more than it can afford." He stood up. "Quiet and careful, now. Do nothing without my permission."

"Why is it so dark?" Zaehr whispered. "And where are the rest of the guards?"

"Asleep, mostly," The voice was jovial, amused. It was Kestal Haladan. "Don't worry, I'll see to it that you're blamed for their unnatural slumber . . . and the deaths of those who don't survive the evening."

The odor of perfume was strong in the air, but Haladan had left his handkerchief behind. Zaehr could smell the odor that had been so faint in their earlier encounter—ash and burning iron. "It's him," she whispered.

Tolar nodded. If he was surprised, he gave no sign of it. "You can surrender now, Haladan. It will be much simpler if you explain this to Dantian yourself."

"I *will* be explaining everything to Dantian," Haladan said, "but we can finish *our* business right here." He gestured, his fingers flickering in an arcane pattern.

Zaehr tried to charge forward, to grapple with him, but even as she started to move she felt a wave of mystical energy flow over her. She froze. Every muscle was rigid. She couldn't even turn her head to look at Tolar.

"I do wish they'd sent a half-orc," Haladan said. "The common people just don't think of House Tharashk when they see a human. And if your house is to take the blame for the shipping attacks *and* this ill-conceived attempt to assassinate Lord Dantian . . . well, a killer with orc blood would have looked much better on the front page of the *Korranberg Chronicle.* Still . . ." He walked over to Zaehr and stroked her chin with one bejeweled finger. "You're something of a monster yourself.

Some sort of sewer beast, aren't you? We're lucky the house defenses stopped you long enough for the guards to put you down."

A short sword lay on a nearby shelf. Haladan picked it up and drew it from its sheath. The steel gleamed in the torchlight, and Zaehr guessed it had never seen use in battle. She struggled to break the spell, but her will was no match for this magic. She could only stand helplessly as Haladan returned with the blade. He put the point to her throat, and Zaehr felt the cold sting of steel pressing through the skin. Then he paused.

"Of course, I suppose it would make a better story if you'd fought me first—the helpless servant showing just how deadly the beast can be." He smiled, and as he did a long, bloody cut stretched down across his cheek. Teeth-marks appeared on his shoulder and right wrist, and bloodstained slits spread across his clothes. "That should do."

"I think we can do better."

Zaehr had been watching Haladan, and for all her remarkable senses she hadn't seen Tolar move; she'd never have guessed the old man was capable of such stealth. But the surprise was far worse for Haladan. Zaehr saw a glint of dark steel in Tolar's hand, and she heard the sound of a blade piercing flesh.

The servant's scream drowned out all other sounds. The howl was deep, undulating, more beast than a man. Spinning around, he grabbed Tolar by the throat and lifted him into the air, displaying an inhuman strength that Zaehr would never have guessed was hidden beneath his flabby flesh. Dark fire flickered around Haladan's fist. Tolar gasped and turned pale. The bloody wound on Haladan's back was quickly healing, as if he was drawing the lifeforce from the old man and using it to rejuvenate himself. With a final curse, Haladan flung Tolar across the hall. The old man slammed into the far wall and slid to the floor.

Zaehr called on every ounce of strength she possessed. She felt her jaws distend as her fangs slid out, but she needed more than the strength of the beast. She reached back to her childhood, calling on the feral monster that had haunted the sewers of Sharn. Back then she'd been more animal than human, driven by pure, primal emotions—fear, hunger, anger. It was that rage that she drew on now, a terrible fury that burned away all thought. The mystical bonds that had held her paralyzed shattered, and she flew forward.

She was upon Haladan in a storm of tooth and steel. She felt a raw visceral thrill as one of her curved blades traced a red streak across her enemy's back. Lunging, she sank her teeth into his neck.

Pain washed over her, a white-hot flash of agony. It was as if she'd bitten a burning log. Haladan's blood was fire, searing her lips and mouth. Pain blinded her, and in that instant Haladan struck.

"You *worm!*" he roared.

Zaehr ducked back, but she wasn't quick enough. The tip of Haladan's blade pierced her leather harness and dug a bloody furrow along her ribs. Blood and pain fogged Zaehr's eyes, but her animal spirit was still with her. Beneath the streets of Sharn, she'd often had to fight her prey in utter darkness, and she let those instincts guide her now. Scent and sound painted a picture that was almost as clear as sight, and she could *feel* her enemy charging her, giving her just enough insight to block his blow. She lashed out with her twin blades, tearing into Haladan's arm.

But something was wrong.

There wasn't enough blood. Her sense of smell painted a picture, and for all the blows Zaehr had landed, Haladan wasn't bleeding. Other smells filled the room—a powerful odor of smoke, of sulphur, threatening to overwhelm her keen senses.

Her vision cleared. She parried a blow from Haladan's blade and lashed at his neck . . . and nearly dropped her blade in surprise.

Haladan was gone.

The portly servant had been replaced by a new figure—a lean, muscular male who held the shortsword with obvious confidence and skill. This stranger was anything but human. He had the head of a fierce jungle cat, and his fangs were larger and longer than Zaehr's. Thick fur covered his body—glossy black fur streaked by bands of rippling fire. These same flames danced in his inhuman eyes. He was beautiful and terrible, a hunter from Zaehr's deepest nightmares. Yet her nose told her that he was also Haladan. His scent was masked by fire and musk, and his old robes had vanished completely—but the traces were still there, ghostly wisps of scent clinging to him like mist.

"What *are* you?" she said, stumbling back and crossing her blades before her.

The stranger laughed, and his voice was like bubbling oil. "I am the darkness. I am fear and I am fire. My kind ruled this world in its infancy, and we—"

"Love the sound of your own voice?" Zaehr hurled both her knives, drawing new blades the instant they left her hands. One of the daggers struck between the monster's eyes. The other sank into his gut.

Whatever this thing was, he didn't have the weaknesses of a man. With a rumbling, oily laugh, he tore the blades from his flesh and flung them back at her. Zaehr spun to the side, but she wasn't fast enough and one of the knives carved a deep gash along her forearm. The monster's wounds began healing the instant he plucked out the knives.

"Fool!" he rumbled. "You cannot harm me with mortal steel. While I can end this with but a touch." Black fire crackled around his fingers, and he strode toward her.

Fear filled Zaehr's mind. But reason fought back. She was no longer the savage child. She was faster than the fiend, and she used her speed, retreating as her mind raced. She remembered her lessons, as Tolar taught her the ways of logic and reason. *Every problem has a solution. Every mystery has an answer.*

Mortal steel.

The dagger Tolar had used—that had certainly caused the creature pain. Whether it was magical or forged of some unearthly metal, it was what she needed. She leaped to the side as the feline monstrosity charged at her, staying inches ahead of his touch. She scoured the room, searching as best as she could while staying in constant motion.

There!

Zaehr pounced, leaping past the fiend and snatching the dagger off the floor. It was made of a dark metal with a reddish sheen, and it felt warm to the touch. She caught sight of some sort of engraving on the blade, but there was no time to study the inscription. Haladan was upon her, and even as she turned she could feel a terrible chill as the dark aura around his hands grazed her shoulder.

"We're all mortal," she said, burying the blade in his heart.

Haladan howled, a cry of agony that echoed the one she'd heard before. Zaehr yanked the blade free, and a fountain of darkness flowed from the wound. The demon dropped to one knee, clutching at his chest with his left hand.

"*No!*" he cried, his voice losing strength with each second. "You . . . destroyed me, creature of dirt."

Zaehr was astonished. *One blow?* She looked down at the knife.

She knew it was a mistake the instant she took her eyes off Haladan. He dived forward, his blade rising in a steel arc. *Fool!* She cursed herself—too late. She started to move back, but he struck with inhuman precision. His blade smashed into—

The crimson dagger.

Fire flashed and thunder rolled. When the smoke cleared both blades had shattered, leaving only blackened shards and twisted hilts. And Haladan's hand was around Zaehr's throat.

"You pathetic creature," he said, lifting her off the ground. "You think to match wits with *me?*"

Zaehr kicked him hard, aiming her blow for a place most men would find difficult to ignore. Haladan simply laughed and tightened his grip on her neck.

"I was there at the dawn of creation. I have played games with your kind since you were rooting in the mud, before you even *knew* how to make fire. You are a pawn on a board so vast you cannot even see the squares." Cold flames flowed around his hand, and Zaehr felt her strength being drawn away. "There was only one creature in this city that I feared, and she—"

"*Was not alone.*" The voice was a thunderclap, and the blow that accompanied it smashed the demon to the ground.

Zaehr fell back against the floor, dazed and weakened by the fiend's touch. She heard terrible sounds, and the smell of sulphur and molten steel swept over her, threatening to drown her senses. She forced herself to her elbows. What she saw made her doubt her reason.

There was a dragon in the chamber, filling the hall behind her.

It was smaller than the massive silver beast that had died in *Pride of the Storm*, but it was still one of the most majestic and terrifying creatures she'd ever seen. About thirty feet from nose to tail, its thick scales were the color of wet blood. Long black horns swept back across its head, and its eyes were pools of flickering light. Vast jaws yawned wide, and fire filled the hall.

Zaehr lay just beneath the dragon's head, and the flames passed over her. This was no natural fire, and the heat was dizzying. Where the flames touched stone the walls *melted*, liquefying and flowing away from the terrible heat. When the light faded, the gates of the Stormwind Keep were gone, melted by the dragon's breath.

The demon was still alive, kneeling amid the cooling stone. The flames had burned away patches of fur and skin, revealing blackened muscle and steaming blood, but he rose to his feet, bearing his fangs in a fierce snarl.

The dragon flowed over Zaehr in a blur of scarlet scales. It smashed into Haladan, hurling the fiend into the empty streets of Oak Towers. The dragon followed, seeming to double in size as it emerged from the blasted entrance and spread its wings.

Whatever Haladan's motives, he had courage. He hurled himself at his foe, lashing out with his dark fists. It was an act of desperation—and futility. Even as Haladan charged, the dragon lashed out with its powerful tail. The blow sent the fiend reeling. The dragon gestured with one claw, and Haladan froze in place. Zaehr could see a rippling field of energy surrounding the fiend, a nearly invisible fist, and as she watched in stunned silence she could hear ribs cracking one by one.

"You . . . you cannot . . . defeat us," Haladan said, burning blood leaking from his mouth. "You are still . . . only mortal. I . . . cannot die."

"Perhaps," the dragon rumbled. "We have held you at bay for a hundred thousand years. The humans, the elves, the shifters . . . they live and prosper, in spite of your games." The dragon clenched its claw, and the fiend hissed in agony. "What are you? You are nothing. A worthless memory of a time long gone. A lord of dust and nothing more. You can kill us, but there will be others waiting to put an end to you. And someday, the younger races will be ready to face you on their own."

"You—" Haladan began, but the dragon was done with conversation. It reached out, and its long black claws sank into the chest of the fiend. The demon's eyes grew wide, and the burning stripes along his fur flared into brilliant light. But the dragon showed no signs of pain, and an instant later Haladan shuddered and was still. The flames along his fur slowly faded.

"Tolar!" Zaehr rolled to her feet, her burned lips drawn back across her fangs. Her companion was nowhere to be seen.

The dragon flung the corpse to the side, a casual gesture that sent the broken body skidding across the cobblestones. It turned to Zaehr, and as it fixed her with its luminous gaze she was gripped by pure, unreasoning terror—the raw panic a mighty predator instills in its prey.

"Tolar had no place in such a battle," the dragon said. Its voice was thunder and steam, a rumbling hiss that Zaehr felt in her bones. Its crimson scales glittered in the torchlight, as if it was painted in fresh blood. This ruddy armor was punctuated by black ivory—two dark horns stretching back of its massive head, and ebon talons longer than any of Zaehr's blades. Even its teeth were dark, as if burned black by the flames that licked around its jaws. But the true fire was in its eyes. The blazing orange orbs consumed her thoughts, reducing her to a frightened child. It took all her strength of will to tear her gaze away, to wrap one hand around the hilt of a curved dagger.

How had it come to this?

"This ends now!" The rumbling voice tore Zaehr back into the present. The knife slid into her hand. Her wounds burned as she fell into a defensive crouch, ready to leap. The dragon towered above her, rearing back on its hind legs, jaws thrown wide. Time slowed to a crawl, and Zaehr could see the light rising in the gullet of the beast.

Fire, she thought. It had begun with fire.

Zaehr woke with a start. The image was still etched in her brain. A second torrent of fire bursting from the lips of the dragon, engulfing the body of the fiend and burning it to ash. The great beast turning to face her, and—

"Feeling better?"

"No." Zaehr sat up and turned to face the speaker. "I don't know why you won't get me another healing potion." Her wounds itched, and it was all she could do to keep from tearing them open.

"Do you know what Jorasco charges for such salves?" Tolar said, setting a cup of steaming tal by the side of the bed. "If I paid for mystical healing every time you hurt yourself, we'd be on the streets within a week."

"I thought dragons slept on mountains of gold."

Tolar's face froze. "The dream again?"

"Yes." She watched him carefully. He hid it well, but she could sense his discomfort every time she brought it up.

The truth was far less exciting than the dream. Her injuries had been worse than she'd thought, and she passed out before reaching the gates of Stormwind Keep. Inside, Tolar had managed to lure Haladan before Lord Dantian and tricked him into confessing before his master. Haladan had used magic to escape, but for the moment Dantian was satisfied. Haladan had been the one seeding his master's thoughts with suspicions of House Tharashk. Now it seemed clear that it was Haladan and his cult that were responsible for the disaster. The danger to Lyrandar shipping might not be over—but at least Lyrandar had a better idea of who was responsible. As for the dead dragon, it remained a mystery. Dantian maintained that it must have been working with his treacherous chief servant, and at the moment, there was no reason to believe otherwise.

But somehow, it still felt . . . wrong. Tolar had taught her to follow patterns, to make sense of the jumble of facts. This seemed too simple, too convenient. After Tolar had left, she found herself lying in bed and thinking about her dream. The images were faint, already fading away, but she could piece together a trail from the faintest hints of scent,

and memories were no different. She thought about an old man with a red beard and coat, a friend who didn't want her to follow him. She pulled together fragments of sound and thought, reconstructing the words the dragon might have said when it turned toward her. . . .

"You should not have come here." The luminous eyes were fixed on her, but she could see that there was no anger in their gaze. This creature might be the world's deadliest predator . . . but she was not its prey.

She lowered her knives. "Tolar?" she said.

"At times."

"Why? Why didn't you tell me?"

"There are only a few of us out in the world, sentinels watching for creatures like Haladan. It will be difficult to repair the damage he has done. My brethren will do what they can to normalize relations between Lyrandar and Tharashk—and to prevent the fiends from destroying more ships. But our role in this cannot be known."

"What am I supposed to believe now? Is King Boranel a dragon? Or just one of his advisors?"

"Power is not what we seek, child. There are ancient nations of my kind, hidden in the land of Argonnessen. If conquest was our goal, your people would never have spread across the land." He let his breath out in a long hiss. "You will stand on your own, one day. But the Lord of the First Flame and the other ancient fiends will always be out there, always seeking vengeance for their defeat. They do not seek power either—just chaos and destruction. Even we are not safe from their evil, as Adaixaliantha's murder shows. So we must work from the shadows. Strike with surprise. Secrecy is our shield and our greatest weapon."

"So what does that mean for me?" Zaehr said.

A long hiss. "By the laws of our kind, you should be killed. You have seen my true face, and I have told you more than you should know."

"You could have told me that part first."

"You should not have followed me. But I have no wish to kill you, child. You . . . you have been a faithful friend, and I have enjoyed our time together. I am not without talents of my own. I can twist a few minutes of memory—difficult magic to work, but within my power. It is what I must do to resolve this matter with Lord Dantian." Fire flashed in the orange eyes. "And if you wish to live, it is what I must do with you."

Zaehr considered. "What do I need to do?"

"It will be best if I render you unconscious, I think.

You will wake on the steps of the keep, with the new memories in place. You should never know what truly happened."

Zaehr raised an eyebrow. "Is this the first time you've done this to me?"

"Do you truly wish to know the answer?"

"I suppose not." Zaehr took a deep breath. "If you're going to make all of this go away, I've got one more question."

"Anything."

"You say you're here to protect us. But are there . . . bad dragons out there? Dragons with other ideas about what we need?"

The dragon stared down at her, smoke trailing from his nostrils.

And that was where the dream ended.

About the Author

Keith Baker discovered DUNGEONS & DRAGONS® in elementary school, and this was the beginning of a lifelong interest in games of all sorts. In 2002 he quit his day job to become a full-time freelance writer. Much to his surprise, in 2003 his world EBERRON™ was selected as the finalist in the Wizards of the Coast Fantasy Setting Search. Keith currently lives in Boulder, Colorado with his lovely wife Ellen and a very bossy cow.

The City of Towers was his first novel. *The Shattered Land* is the sequel.

About the Artist

Michael Komarck was born in Louisiana and promptly relocated to Michigan where he has lived ever since. As the years passed, he transitioned from crayons to pencils to acrylics to oils, and in 1989 he found himself at a community college where his suspicions that he was better off self-taught in art where proven correct almost immediately. His stint there was brief in the extreme.

After several years as a projectionist at the local Cineplex, Komarck co-founded a small publishing company. However, with the exception of illustrating several children's books, the majority of his time was spent designing business cards, ads, and eventually web related materials. It was during this period that he was introduced to Photoshop and ultimately replaced his oils with digital paint. Eventually he left to pursue a career as a full time illustrator. He spent a couple years building a portfolio while designing business/self-help book covers to pay the bills (to this day he still happily design several such covers a year).

91

Unnatural Predator

Vaan felt his master drawing near long before there were visible signs. He had spent his entire life serving the dragon ... but it wasn't familiarity that guided the blue pixie's eyes skyward. Duty and fear bound Vaan to his master as deeply as any magic, and he felt the great beast's approach as a mouse feels the shadow of a hawk.

The sky throbbed as the dragon swooped down from the pre-dawn clouds. It was gigantic—over one hundred feet long—and as lean and sinuous as a serpent. Its head was as broad and sharp as an axe-blade, and its long alabaster horns jutted forward beyond the end of its tapering snout. His master was awesome—a beautiful sight even after decades of servitude, and Vaan cursed himself for being swayed by it.

And yet, what a majestic monster to be enslaved by. Its scales were an exquisite fused glass, blue-white in color and harder than steel. A small dot of light glowed in each scale's center like a candle through a translucent ceramic jug. The dragon had wide, sweeping, batlike wings veined with subtle shades of cyan and yellow. As the

by SCOTT MCGOUGH

MAGIC
The Gathering™

great serpent flew, the colors on its wings shimmered and merged. Last night's lingering moon glistened across the brute's streamlined body, enveloping it in a cloud of silver sparks.

Two streams of thick smoke trailed from its nostrils, braiding together as the dragon rolled. The titan's jagged wings carried it over the wooded countryside below, soaring east toward the rain-swollen river.

Vaan's rush of admiration soured as he watched the dragon descend. As surely as he knew his master was approaching, Vaan also knew where the beast was going.

"It's happening again," the pixie whispered, surprising himself by speaking aloud. If the others heard him they gave no sign. Considering the scene that now played out before them, it was understandable how they could overlook the muttered ramblings of a small winged man hovering overhead.

Far below them all, dozens of human figures scurried across the sturdy wooden bridge that spanned the river. Four straight days of driving rain had gorged the river to the point of catastrophe, though the levees remained intact. The local farmers and villagers, wisely unwilling to risk the flood that would greet them if the levees failed, marched across the bridge and continued up the heavily wooded hills to the west. The bridge took three generations of hard work to complete, along with a significant chunk of the hardwood forest nearby. For decades it provided the farmers and village merchants with access to the western lands across the river. Now it provided a way for them to reach higher ground and safety.

Consumed with escaping the rising water with their families and valuables intact, the locals failed to see the even greater danger descend from above. The dragon undulated its body as it flew, swimming through thick streams of cold air and high wind, its eyes fixed on the people below.

Vaan's tongue was a block of stone in his mouth—he could say nothing, do nothing. Nothing except stand, wait, and watch like the loyal servant he was bound to be.

The dragon's brilliant eyes crackled, and tiny jags of blue and yellow energy danced across its face. Its gaze locked on the heavy wooden bridge and the refugees lurching across it. The beast opened its jaws and arched its back, spreading its wings to slow its descent and steady its aim. Its spiked tail curled under its feet, and the dragon hovered in place, its huge wings churning the water below.

The beast drew its long neck back, and a dull boom sounded from within its chest. Its lower neck swelled like a frog's to grotesque, almost comical proportions, then the bulge surged up the dragon's throat to its mouth and erupted in a halo of white light.

The dragon lunged like a striking adder and coughed out a glowing sphere of white-hot energy. The sphere coalesced into a solid ball of electric fire and hurtled down toward the western end of the bridge. Dropping like a comet, the crackling missile plowed through the bridge's wet wood pilings and into the heavy clay below.

Vaan's lips parted, but only a faint wheeze emerged. Another moment passed as the farmers stood frozen, glancing nervously at each other. Then the western end of the bridge exploded.

People, water, and debris were cast hundreds of yards in every direction. Before the first victims landed, the dragon coughed out another blast and the east end of the bridge vanished in a cloud of splinters, foam, and jagged light. Those refugees who weren't killed outright or hurled from the bridge were trapped in the middle of the river on an unstable island of cracked, groaning wood.

Instead of pressing its attack, the brute rose higher, circled back, and cut a great, looping arc across the sky. It rolled and spun as it soared, insouciant and careless, as if it had forgotten its unfinished work below.

But the beast soon veered back toward the villagers and the bridge. It swooped so close to the river's surface its tail carved tiny wakes in the water. The dragon stretched the rest of its body out long and straight as it homed in on the final section of intact bridge. While dozens of tiny figures remained atop the crumbling structure, very few were moving—many of those still conscious fell to their knees and covered their heads.

The wind whistled against the dragon's scales, rasping over their razor edges with a stinging, sharp sound. The beast bore down on the bridge, its eyes glowing yellow and blue and its face fixed in a feral grin.

The dragon's head dipped and broke the surface of the river. Ignoring the sheer force of the river's flow, the dragon slipped under water a mere hundred yards from its target. Vaan shuddered at the beast's casual display of grace and power—the winged devil had disappeared into the raging water as smoothly as a child easing into a bathtub from its mother's arms.

For an endless moment there was no sign of the beast. Lightning continued to slice through the clouds overhead, the river continued to rush and froth, and the remnants of the shattered bridge continued to teeter and burn, but the creature's attack had once more stopped as suddenly and capriciously as it had started. No one was lulled by the trick a second time, but Vaan knew why the beast had played it twice: it delighted in their realization that even though they knew what was about to happen, there was nothing they could do to stop it.

Finally, a horned, scaly head burst up from below the center of the bridge, scattering planks and farmers like drops of water from a shaking dog. The dragon craned its supple neck through and over the remnants of the bridge and turned its terrible eyes on the dazed survivors. Contemptuously, the great beast hissed, shrugged, and drew its muscular neck partially back under the ruined structure.

Then, with a brutal surge of power, it forced most of its body through the head-sized hole it had made. Timbers shattered and boulders flew as the last of the bridge's foundations splintered, then slowly collapsed into the water. The debris quickly broke apart and was carried away by the water, and the farmers' screams finally gurgled to a sickening halt as the last of the bridge's pilings disappeared into the deluge.

The dragon slithered onto solid ground and rose up on its thick hind legs. At its full height the beast undulated again, ripples of muscle cascading along the length of its body under its glistening ceramic armor. Its magnificent scales stood on end, quivering in the moonlight as tiny arcs of galvanic energy sparked between them.

The great beast spread its wings wide and with two powerful beats rose into the air. Two more long, languid beats took the dragon back to the edge of the clouds. It huffed and snorted as it rose ever higher, and smoke trailed from its nostrils. Vaan grimly marked the evidence of the dragon's visit to the farmland below: three score dead, two wisps of thick smoke, and the shattered remains of an entire community.

The dragon itself made no such accounting as it soared toward the largest peak on the eastern horizon, not sparing a backward glance at the evening's entertainment.

It's happening again, Vaan thought, careful this time to keep silent. But soon I will finally see it end.

Tania Cayce stared after the dragon as the monster flew away. She was crouched and silent, safely concealed (they assured her) by a thick sheaf of leaves and the cold morning mist.

Cayce did not feel safe. In her mind, awe fought for supremacy against terror and self-preservation, so there was very little room for comforting thoughts of safety. Her heart beat painfully in her chest, and she was unable to remember why she had come here in the first place—or why she wasn't running for her life. She peered at the obscene wreck the dragon had made of both the bridge and the people on it. She realized she was at least better off than the poor devils down there. She was alive, for one thing, and for another it wasn't raining up here on the mountainside.

"That is our quarry," the female guide said. She was huge, six and a half feet tall, and dressed as a wild woman from the forest with hide clothing and bone fetishes. Her eyes were almost vibrating in her head, and a huge grin stretched her features. Her partner, a small male pixie, hovered silent and dour beside her on dragonfly wings.

"We will test this dragon's strength, its cunning, and its essential right to be," the woman continued. "If we are resolute, and if our cause is righteous—"

"It is," said a softer voice from the procession ahead, "but vengeance will be served, be we righteous or not."

From behind Cayce and from ahead of her came the murmured assent of soldiers. Directly in front of her, Master Rus turned and beckoned her closer. Cayce scooted forward and turned her head so her ear was next to her mentor's mouth.

"I hate working with fanatics," Rus whispered. "Especially religious and military ones. Still," the stout man said. "That moping blue bugger's plan is sound. And the rewards will be well worth the risk." He took Cayce by the chin and turned her face so that their eyes met.

"Don't look so concerned," Rus said. He was not warm or comforting but stern, determined to banish any chance his apprentice's expression had of reflecting badly on him. Potionmaster Donner Rus was known throughout five kingdoms as a poisoner without peer, and he valued that reputation above all else. Three of the five monarchs he worked with kept him on permanent retainer to prevent him from using his craft on them, and Master Rus was very fond of being paid for not doing his dangerous work.

This time, however, Master Rus had accepted a massive fee for his personal attention in the matter of slaying a dragon. Cayce knew her master was unlikely to admit it, but Rus had taken this job largely to salve his bruised ego. Vaan the pixie had let fly a torrent of subtle barbs about the Potionmaster's age and fading glory—if Master Rus wanted to redeem his reputation and save face, he had to either take the job or take offense. Cayce kept this observation to herself, of course. Any apprentice who volunteered such information would not remain healthy, sane, or in Rus's service for long.

Now Master Rus spoke firmly, the tone of a professional talking about his business. "You know what your master requires, Tania, and you shall provide it. Stay close behind me; be quick with what I ask for; and remember the most important thing artists like us must do, with excellence, at all times." He prompted Cayce with a tilt of his head.

"Observe and be silent." Cayce bobbed a quick bow and felt her eyes drying. Her master had a way of looking at Cayce that made her forget to blink. Also, she was unwilling to take her eyes off the old devil for long, lest he slip her a dose of something nasty. She forced herself to blink and felt a dry, sandy pop as her eyelids met.

"Very good." Rus turned away and continued up the trail. The stout man quickly caught up to the soldiers without deigning to visibly rush. Cayce fell in behind her master, sticking close enough to hear his asides but well clear of his billowing satin cape.

The guides led them on, approaching the dragon's lair from the south. Both the forest woman and the somber pixie assured them that though this path was steeper and more treacherous than the northern route, it was also more heavily wooded and would be shrouded in mist until midday. They could expect to climb halfway up the mountain before the dragon had any chance of spotting them . . . provided the party members all kept their footing and didn't plummet to their deaths.

Cayce shifted her heavy pack and tucked a strand of long white hair back into her headdress. She had seen and done many strange things apprenticing with Master Rus, from harvesting graveyard mushrooms by moonlight to milking spiders with tweezers. Sometimes the things she saw and did came back to her while she slept, and she awoke with a half-strangled scream in her throat.

This trek up the mountain was something new, however. Even the lurid drudgery one found as a poisoner's apprentice could not compare to participating in an actual dragon hunt. She had never imagined such a thing in her most fevered dreams, not even in those brought on by the most toxic fumes from her master's cauldron.

In addition to her private misgivings, Cayce felt the guides were surely the most discouraging pair anyone had ever followed up a dark mountain. Vaan, the morose blue-haired pixie, had the body of a grown man at just under half the size. Alone, he seemed perfectly proportioned, handsome even, with his white eyes shimmering like smoke, but with someone beside him to provide a sense of scale, he was stunted and absurd.

Atypically for a pixie, Vaan spoke little, brooded often, and seemed perpetually on the verge of sighing. He seemed detached from his own quest for freedom—oddly disinterested in the mission he had hired them to perform.

When they asked him why he and the forest woman had formed the party and were leading it to the dragon, Vaan muttered something about his people being conquered and generations of slavery under the wily old serpent's cruel yoke. It was a listless tale told without enthusiasm, and it was neither inspiring nor convincing.

For all his good looks and purportedly noble motives, Cayce found Vaan empty and pathetic. To her, he seemed like a sad miniature statue, an artist's study in melancholy done in sharp-cut gems and blue-tinged marble.

The female guide was named Kula, and while she was more formidable looking than the pixie, she was no more encouraging. Kula did all the talking once the journey was underway, and she seemed to know her way around the woods that surrounded the dragon's mountain. A braided band of tough, woody vine held her hair tight against her broad skull, almost disappearing against the backdrop of her nut-brown skin. Kula claimed to be an anchorite, which she further defined as some sort of religious hermit.

Cayce was happy to agree. In fact, she was happy to grant Kula any title, so long as the huge woman didn't wad Cayce up like a pinch of fresh bread and swallow her whole.

Cayce wasn't only disconcerted by Kula's size. Kula's hulking form was a mild amusement compared to the reverential, almost trancelike state she entered when she spoke of killing dragons. As an anchorite, Kula claimed to be a student of nature and an agent of the natural order. Her role, she said, was to enforce the laws of the jungle. Confronting the dragon in its nest was a spiritual trial she was undertaking, a holy effort made to advance her on the path to enlightenment.

This peculiar attitude seemed to make Kula cold and aloof toward Cayce and her master. Cayce was not quite sure why. Some of the most effective poisons were completely organic, derived from the natural creatures and plants that lived in Kula's forest.

The rest of the ten-member party was rounded out by a small squad of soldiers: one officer, four infantry, and one golem. The officer introduced himself as Captain Allav Hask, and though his face was dead and waxy, his eyes burned with cold fury. He wore one sword on his hip that seemed normal enough, and one strapped across his back that was clearly for special occasions. This grander, larger sword was sheathed in a gleaming golden scabbard and wrapped in multiple layers of fresh white linen. The wrappings came loose as they hiked, giving Cayce the chance to note the powerful runes carved into the sword's scabbard and hilt. What would happen, she wondered, when the captain drew that enchanted blade?

Captain Hask always kept two of his infantry close by him at the front of the party, just behind the guides. The other two brought up the rear, both to protect them all from attack and to make sure the heavy golem kept up.

Kula was massive and Vaan was as dour as stone, but the golem was literally a massive

statue. The soldiers called the stone man "it" or "the golem" when the captain was in earshot, but among themselves they called him "Boom." He was carved in the rough outline of a man with only the vaguest and most rudimentary features. The reddish granite of his body glowed softly at the shoulder and neck joints, and his heavy brow jutted out over two hollow, smoking eye sockets. When he opened his mouth to acknowledge the captain's orders Cayce could see, hear, and smell the inferno burning inside.

Boom the golem seemed mindless—utterly devoid of a personality or independent thought. Judging from what she had seen so far, Cayce guessed he wasn't designed for such niceties. Along the route she had watched him crush a chunk of granite to powder beneath his feet and bend back a foot-thick evergreen as though it were a stalk of corn. No military or mechanical expert, Cayce nonetheless guessed Boom was built for close-quarters combat where brute power and durability were more important than speed and tactical thinking.

Of them all, Master Rus himself was the most familiar figure, but to Cayce he was alien and strange to begin with and thus seemed so in every context. Rus was dressed as always in inappropriate finery that managed to seem both formal and flamboyant. His wide-brimmed black hat was rimmed with a curtain of golden yarn strands that hung down over his eyes and danced against the tip of his round nose. He wore an ornate ruby ring and carried a polished hardwood walking stick with a sharp-faceted crystal skull on the handle. The purple satin lining of his cape glinted in the waning moonlight when the wind whipped it open.

Rus carried nothing but his cane, leaving Cayce to bear their food, water, and dozens of arcane substances carefully organized in jars, bottles, and pouches. Her master claimed to have bested dragons before, but Rus was such a liar and a braggart that Cayce never knew when he was being sincere and when he was just selling himself to a customer. In any case, she knew he had brought along his deadliest potions and powders, and the knowledge that they were at least well-armed lightened her load considerably.

Ahead, Kula motioned for the party to stop. They were approaching the edge of the tree line and, according to the anchorite, were "about to venture into the most exposed and dangerous part of the journey." When outlining the plan at the base of the mountain, Kula had paused before adding, "Barring its end, of course, where battle with the dragon itself may prove more dangerous." As she said this, Kula had almost swooned behind a dreamy, unfocused grin.

Cayce despaired at the sight of the tree line. She silently cursed her own pessimism, wishing she could do as Master Rus often bade her and see advantages and opportunities instead of dangers and consequences. Cayce did not voice this thought to her master because doing so in the past had only caused Rus to lecture her, and if there was one thing Rus loved, it was lecturing.

"Great poisoners see only opportunity," he'd say. "If you want to limit your vision to avoiding threats and consequences instead of delivering them . . . if you want to defend instead of taking the initiative, at least do it properly. There's always a market for royal food-tasters, though their careers don't usually last long enough for them to distinguish themselves. Especially when Master Rus is on the job."

As the rest of the party gathered around Kula to hear the plan reviewed once more, Rus made a show of being bored. He wandered off a few paces, still within earshot but not part of the semicircle around Kula. Cayce watched Vaan hovering moodily behind the forest woman.

Something about the two of them together jarred Cayce from her private thoughts. The pixie seemed impatient and hesitant at the same time, both anxious to proceed and fearful of what they had yet to encounter. Kula, for her part, seemed eager to begin their mission, but there was something grudging about the way she spoke to the others—as if she were unwilling to share this rare opportunity. Cayce watched Vaan brood as Kula quietly but fiercely outlined their plan of attack. The guides' demeanor and Cayce's general dislike of the entire situation nagged at her until an important truth became painfully clear to her.

All one had to do was look at their faces. The guides had assembled the party and they were leading the party into action. The pixie was full of hope and dread, and the anchorite was full of anticipation and selfish longing. In contrast, the soldiers were all grim and focused, perhaps bent on avenging some attack or another the beast had visited upon their nation. To a man they showed nothing more than determination. Master Rus's expression showed only a preoccupation with his appearance. To him it was just another job, another chance to improve his reputation and his standing among the kingdoms' aristocrats.

Only the guides seemed to have concrete expectations about the party's date with the dragon. What did they know that gave them such feelings? What did they know that they hadn't shared? Whatever it was, it was something Cayce, Rus, and the rest of them did not know, and it would be unprofessional to let them keep it that way.

"Master," Cayce whispered as she walked.

Rus slowed ahead of her, pretending to struggle as he extracted the tip of his cane from a crack in the rocks. "What is it?"

"I have been observing, as you have taught me. I think I have identified an opportunity."

Master Rus stopped twisting his cane and cocked an eyebrow at Cayce. "Spreading our wings, Apprentice? Expanding our horizons?" Rus chuckled softly, but he was interested. "Is this an opportunity for knowledge, profit, or advancement?"

"For survival," Cayce said. She cast her eyes toward the guides then back to her master. "Remember how you once told me never to work with pixies? They always talk too much, you said. They always give away the game

and tip off the target because they can't keep secrets to themselves."

Rus scowled. "That was sprites," he said. "Or faeries. I never said anything about pixies." He quickly glanced at Vaan, then added, "Besides, I need to make that little blue turd eat what he said. Asking me if age has 'softened my resolve as it has my belly.' We'll see how clever he is when Rus the dragon-slayer is a hero among his own people."

Rus's jaw clenched and he yanked the tip of his cane free. "Sprites. Yes, it was definitely sprites. I remember it clearly now. Never work with sprites. They give the whole game away."

"Yes, Master Rus."

"Sprites are smaller than pixies. And even flightier. They burst into song at inappropriate times." Master Rus nodded knowingly, his gaze turned inward. "Pixies are fine as long as they're in front of you. As long as you remember they're steeped in glamour."

"Yes, Master Rus."

Rus worked his jaw. Cayce forced herself to blink.

"Fine," he said. "You have Master Rus's attention. What have you seen?"

Cayce leaned in close to Rus's ear. "Vaan said hardly anything beyond his needling insults. And he hasn't talked to anyone much at all since we met him. Is that typical pixie behavior?"

Rus planted the tip of his cane and swirled his cape dramatically around his arm. "It is not. You believe he knows more than he's saying?"

"He must."

"And so we ought to know more of what he knows."

"That or we should walk away. You've taught me that much," Cayce said.

Rus nodded. "I'm not walking away, and neither are you."

"No, Master."

"But I do think you're on to something. I've never seen a more downtrodden pixie, even if he does bear a slavery-fueled tale of woe."

"Shall we brace him, Master? Confront him and draw out what he's hiding? I have an idea—"

"Not we," Rus said. "You. Pursue your idea, Apprentice. Without my help. Brace the pixie on your own, and Master Rus will stand back and observe." Rus cocked another eyebrow at her. "Think of this as an impromptu examination. A field test of your practical skills."

Cayce hesitated, seeking a hidden snare in Rus's offer. Her master gathered his cape around his shoulders and leaned on his cane.

"Well?" He tipped his hat toward the rest of the party, segments of golden yarn waving before his eyes. "Begin."

Cayce took a deep breath and went forward. She sidled up alongside one of the soldiers and waited for Kula to pause for breath.

"Captain Hask's golem being the last line of frontal attack. Which brings us to …" Kula looked up from the map she was scrawling on the ground and nodded to Cayce. "Nice of you to join us. If the golem proves necessary, you and your master must be standing by, ready to—"

"How do we know it's the right dragon?" Cayce said.

Kula blinked. "What?" The anchorite's face and voice were edged with annoyance.

"The dragon you're leading us to. How do we know it's the one you hired us to kill?"

"Little girl," the forest woman said as she rose to her full height and planted her fists on her massive hips. "How many marauding dragons have you seen tonight?"

The soldiers laughed, but Cayce remained stoic. "Just one," she said. "The one that attacked the farmers on the bridge. Is that the one?"

"Of course it is, you silly child." Kula called out to Rus, "Master poisoner, would you rein in your student? We're trying to—"

"What color is the dragon Vaan gathered us to hunt?"

Kula paused mid-reply. Instead of answering right away, the anchorite cleared her throat and glanced at Vaan. Then Kula said, "Blue-white, almost silver, like winter lightning. Like moonlight on the edge of a sword. What are you getting at? You saw it yourself, as did we all."

Cayce turned to Vaan. "What color is the dragon we're hunting?"

Vaan could only smile helplessly. After a long pause, he shrugged like a gambler who has just seen his horse come up lame.

"Well?" Cayce said. "You're our patron and our guide, but you don't know the answer? We're trusting you, and you can't even describe the monster that enslaved you and all your people?" Sensing victory, Cayce pressed on. "Let's try something easier. What color is the dragon that wrecked the bridge?"

Vaan and Kula looked at each other uncomfortably.

"Blue-white, almost silver," Kula said crossly.

"So it was." Cayce nodded. "But I asked him."

Vaan merely smiled the same helpless smile and shook his head.

Cayce turned to Captain Hask, hooking her thumb back at Vaan. "He's enchanted," she said. "He can't tell us about the dragon he wants us to kill. He can't even describe it to us after we've all seen it. Think about it. Has he ever said anything concrete to any of us about our quarry?"

Some of the soldiers flickered their eyes toward Captain Hask, and one even coughed, but no one disagreed with her, so Cayce went on.

"That's why he's so quiet all the time, and why she says so much about his job. For all we know, he works for the dragon and it's his job

to lure mice like us into his master's hunting ground."

"No," Vaan said. His face was flushed, and his eyes were wet with rage.

"I can vouch for Vaan," Kula said. "He has told the truth: He is enslaved, and he wants the dragon dead. I would know if he were lying to me."

"So you say, but aren't pixies expert liars? Steeped in illusion and glamour? How would we know if he fooled you? Assuming you're not in on it." Cayce soon regretted this last part as Kula turned her angry eyes on the poisoner's apprentice.

"This is no trick," the anchorite said. "Was it pretense when the dragon destroyed your garrison, Captain Hask? Did lies or sleight of hand destroy the farmers on that bridge? The beast we saw tonight is the same one that attacked your fortress, Captain, the same one that enslaved Vaan's tribe. It is the same one that's been upsetting the natural balance all the way from here to the far edge of my forest. Vaan sought out those of us who have the motivation and the skills necessary to kill this dragon. There will be great danger, but that is no secret. It's also why you and your leering master are being so well paid."

Kula stepped forward, looking past Cayce to Rus. "Is that what this is about? Are you sending in your underling to renegotiate the terms of our agreement?"

Rus started as if Kula's call had woken him from a deep sleep. Slowly, he stretched and yawned, displaying his cape's purple lining in its glorious entirety.

"Sorry, what?" he said. "I was lost in thought. Has my apprentice been speaking out of turn again?"

Kula glanced back at the apprentice. "She has."

"Oh, dear. Did she say anything of substance?"

Cayce held her tongue as her face reddened. Rus was a worm, but surely even he wouldn't just set her up then abandon her like this.

Kula's eyes narrowed, and she looked from Rus, to Cayce, to Hask, to Vaan. The pixie lowered his face, and Kula nodded. "She raised an issue that bears addressing. Vaan is, in fact, under a geas. He is magically prohibited from betraying any of the dragon's secrets. He can say nothing that would cause his master to be harmed."

Rus showed exaggerated interest. "Is he, now? How fascinating. How's that work, then?"

Kula spared one final glare for Cayce before she answered. "The dragon we hunt can exert powerful influence over the minds of sentient beings. Vaan is free to go where he likes when his master doesn't need him, but he can not speak freely of the dragon. Not its nature, not its weaknesses." Kula turned and sneered at Cayce. "Not even its color."

Rus rolled his cane back and forth across his hand. "And you didn't think this was worth mentioning to the hunters you'd assembled? You don't think someone who cannot tell all he knows might have omitted something crucial to our understanding of the stakes? Crucial to our survival?"

"I want him dead," Vaan said. As he spoke, his four transparent wings extended from his back and began to beat. The pixie floated off the ground until he was hovering several feet over the group. "It took me almost a full year to get around the geas and enlist Kula's aid, and only then because she is so intuitive. I did not create this threat. I did not lure you here to be his victims. I did not assemble you for any reason but those Kula voiced on my behalf."

Captain Hask stepped forward, between Kula and Cayce. "None of this is important," he said. "The brute we saw tonight is the one that killed most of my men. I mean to destroy it in its lair or die trying." The officer turned his dead eyes up to Vaan. "Do you know where that dragon nests?"

Vaan shrugged, and Hask said, "I'll take that silence as a yes." He turned to Kula and said, "Can you lead us there?"

"I can, and I will. There is nothing I want more than to confront and defeat this abomination."

"Then I submit—" Hask's glower went back and forth from Cayce to her master—"that its color is immaterial. As is its name, its place of origin, and who can speak freely about it.

"We know what it is. We have seen it in battle. We have all come to kill it. Let's find the damned thing and get on with our work."

Rus paused, stroked his chin, then nodded. "I suppose I must agree. This new information doesn't really change things that much. Stand back and be silent, my apprentice.

When Rus agrees to terms, he sticks to them until the job is done."

Rus's eyes locked on Cayce's from behind his curtain of golden yarn. If Rus's furtive expression wasn't enough to alert her, the colossal lie about never changing a contract's terms would have done the trick. She knew her master was too experienced and too professional to wink, but she recognized his need for her to let this matter drop.

Kula crouched back down over her map in the dirt and said, "We'll reach the edge of its lair just after dawn. The tunnel will lead us all the way to the mountain's interior. We'll wait for the light here, just outside its sense of smell. When the sun burns off the morning fog, we'll go forward in stages, as agreed." She raised her head and locked eyes with Cayce. "And we are still agreed, aren't we? Poisoners?"

"Agreed," Rus called airily.

Cayce bowed her head and stared at Kula's map on the ground.

"Agreed," she said.

Cayce shuddered under the prodding hand of her master. Rus shook her shoulder, drawing her from the deep morass of sleep.

"Come on," he said. "We're leaving."

"Mmm?" Cayce struggled to fully open her eyes. How had she fallen asleep? The last thing she remembered was waiting in the thick brush, just a ridgeline away from a clear view of the dragon's cave.

Rus's thick index finger flicked across Cayce's nose. "Faster than that," he said. His voice was soft and low, just above a whisper. "Let's get what I came for and leave these heroes to their noble work."

Her nose stinging, Cayce rubbed her eyes and swallowed a yawn. "What?"

"What, Master."

"What . . . Master?"

Rus pulled Cayce to her knees and helped her keep her balance when she swayed and almost toppled.

"I was right about pixies," he said. "Never work with 'em. This is a fool's errand, and we're leaving."

Cayce's mind began to clear. She noticed a strong sent of camphor mixed with ammonia in the air around them and the clean, sharp scent of mint from her master's hand.

"But the job?" she managed.

"Stuff the job," Rus said. "If they all get killed, we'll be famous as the only survivors. If they kill the dragon, we can claim to have been a part of it. There's no need to actually get involved."

Cayce shook her head. "The pixie and the anchorite. Boom and the soldiers . . ."

"All asleep. Well, all but the golem, but he can't make a move without his handlers. They'll all stay asleep for another hour or so." Rus grinned wickedly. "I made a small fire downwind of us. Tossed in a few herbs and things you haven't learned about yet. The breeze carried the smoke right to where our party waited." He held out a small sprig of rounded green leaves. "A whiff of this clovermint brings one right out of it. Pity I didn't bring enough for everyone. Now get up. I want to get moving."

Cayce felt the numbness draining out of her arms and legs. "What about our fee, Master?"

"Stuff the fee. We can offset the cost of this little outing and make ourselves a fine profit without so much as a cross word passing between us and the dragon."

Now fully awake, Cayce felt a chill as she weighed Rus's words. "We can?"

"Of course. You didn't really think I would come along on this suicide mission for a handful of pixie's gold and the ephemeral promise of sharing the big serpent's treasure? Which, by the way, we'd never live to spend?

"No, Tania, what I have in mind will keep clients and royalty alike begging at our door for years to come. Now, stop asking questions and attend me."

Cayce struggled to her feet. "Yes, Master Rus. What do you require?"

"Grab your pack and follow. I'll explain on the way." Rus hummed a breezy tune as he swept out of Kula's makeshift camp, nimbly stepping over and around sleeping soldiers. Boom the golem stood and smoldered, perhaps unaffected by Rus's sleeping vapors but unable to take action without direct orders to do so. Both Vaan and Kula dozed among the roots of a scrawny ash tree.

Cayce wrapped her still-clumsy fingers around her pack and hoisted it onto her shoulder. She was trying to make as little noise as possible, but her master had done his work

well. From their placid faces and softly rising chests, she reckoned the dragon could burst from the ground beneath the hunting party's feet and they would not even stir.

Master Rus moved quickly when he wasn't posturing for clients. Recently woozy and burdened as Cayce was, she actually had to struggle to keep up with her rotund mentor. By the time they cleared the final ridge before the dragon's cave, Cayce was red-faced and out of breath.

Rus was waiting for her, crouched behind a jagged boulder. The stony spire jutted from the ground among a dozen similar rock formations. The spires were broken and charred as if by lightning, and the ground below them was flat, cracked, and hard. Rus motioned for Cayce to crouch beside him, his eyes fixed on the hollow depression where the blasted ground met the sheer south face of the mountain.

Cayce crept behind Rus's boulder and lowered her pack. The ground sloped down toward the depression and into a ragged hole that lay almost hidden in the shadows. According to Kula and Vaan, the hole led to a tunnel they could follow right to the edge of the dragon's innermost sanctuary. Both the opening and the tunnel were big enough to accommodate a large serpentine dragon, so they could certainly handle a small party of warriors bent on destroying one.

Cayce looked up to where morning sunbeams glittered through the snowmelt. Ascent up the south face would test the most experienced mountaineer, but a climb was never part of the attack. Kula's plan had been to creep in and confront the dragon head-on, but that plan was asleep with Kula and the others. Now only Rus knew what Rus planned to do. Or rather, what Rus planned for Cayce to do.

Still fixed on the mountainside, Master Rus said, "So you really believed I let that pixie goad me into joining this farce? You must think me an awful fool, my apprentice."

Here it comes, Cayce thought. She expected Rus would chastise her for correctly citing his own advice about pixies, especially since the only retort he had was to claim he had meant sprites. She had no idea what he would put her through for this, though—for assuming he was every inch the overstuffed, egocentric child he played in front of clients.

But there was no malice in Rus this time. Instead, there was a lilt in his voice and a mischievous twinkle in his eye. Still just above a whisper, he fell into the practiced cadence of a master delivering a lecture. "It is good to be thought a fool by one's enemies, Tania. It makes them careless and overconfident.

"But it is less desirable to be thought so by one's students." He grinned. "Especially in the field. So watch and listen as Rus demonstrates why he is Master. I knew the pixie's story didn't smell right. I also knew it didn't matter, not a jot. That little blue weevil and the wild-eyed giantess could have told us we were going to pray the dragon away and I would have cheerfully come along. I am always happy to follow the client's lead . . . at least from the time I accept the retainer to when my own ends take precedence.

"No, all I ever wanted or expected from this engagement was free guide service and an armed escort to the dragon's nest. This created an opportunity, see? There's that word again. An opportunity for someone like you to perhaps harvest certain rare and hard-to-acquire ingredients? Ingredients that someone such as me could perhaps put to especially good use?" The poisoner chuckled, his belly shaking in concert with the shimmering yarn on his hat.

Cayce remained silent too long, and Rus snapped, "Remember your lessons, Apprentice. How many rare and exquisite poisons are derived from dragons?"

Cayce's mind whirled, and she blinked. "Dozens," she said. "Dragon's blood can be brewed into a tasteless, odorless—"

"I said remember your lessons, not recite them. We don't need anything as precious as blood. If we wanted blood I'd have gone along with that forest woman's attack." Rus shook his head. "Blood," he said derisively. "Why don't we just try for the dragon's living heart or both its eyes? No. Scales, teeth, and claws will do for us. Dragons slough off and replace them regularly. If we can collect even a small handful of these from the mouth of the cave, we'll be among the most feared and well-compensated poisoners in the world."

One small fragment of Rus's earlier oration stuck in Cayce's mind. "Master," she whispered. "Someone like me will collect the ingredients?"

"Someone like you, yes. Someone exactly like you. You, in fact." Rus's eyes twinkled merrily. "You, precisely you, exactly you, and only you."

Rus lifted his cane and pried the crystal skull off the end with a wheezing grunt. "I'll loan you this, of course," he said. "If the dragon or one of its minions comes for you, crack the crystal and toss it to the ground between you and the enemy. It releases a miasma that melts living tissue on contact, so if they come any closer they'll dissolve."

Cayce dully stretched out her cupped hands. "Minions," she muttered.

Rus tilted his palm so that the skull rolled into Cayce's outstretched hands. She closed both fists around the grinning purple totem.

Rus presented his gloved fist to Cayce so that the bright red ring was mere inches from her nose. In a flash of motion he opened his hand and plucked the jeweled ring off. "This"—he held it out for Cayce to accept—"is for you personally. If it comes to close quarters, punch this stone into the dragon's body. Anywhere will do. It delivers a toxic jolt powerful enough to kill almost anything. That's the theory, at least. It's never been properly tested, but I have seen it work on a medium-sized hill giant.

"If you can't get in one good punch, put the gem in your mouth and bite down."

Cayce took the ring. "What will that do?"

"It will make your body so toxic that the dragon will keel over after a single bite. A single taste with the tongue, actually, or a single sniff." Rus dusted his gloved hands against each other. "At the very least it will make him sick long enough for me to escape."

Cayce stared at the ring suspiciously. "Thank-you, Master."

"Not at all. It is a sacrifice I am willing to make for you, my apprentice." Rus's eyes grew stern. "Put on the ring."

"Yes, Master Rus." Cayce nodded grimly. She slid the ring on to her thickest finger, where it spun freely. "Master?"

"Mmm?"

"Afterward? If I survive biting the ring, when does the toxic effect wear off?"

"Afterward?" Rus shrugged. "At that point 'afterward' is not really a practical concern, believe you me.

"Now. Duty calls, and you do not have time to waste." Rus pointed at Cayce's burden. "Empty your pack and leave the gear here with me. Go into yonder cave and scoop up as many scales as you can. I expect at least one full load before I'll be ready to leave."

"Yes, Master Rus."

"As for the claws and teeth, I don't expect

you to find any this far out. If you survive long enough to collect and deliver a full pack of scales, we'll know it's safe to venture in deeper. I'd say one . . . no, two hundred yards. Two hundred yards, or two claws, or one tooth. Achieve one of these milestones and you can return." Rus smiled. "I won't make you delve any deeper to see if there are eggs. Dragons are notoriously defensive of their progeny. We could live off the proceeds of a dragon egg for ten lifetimes, but I'd rather have a small fortune and a long life than a huge fortune and no life." Rus pondered a moment. "Though if you see any eggshells, by all means pick them up."

Cayce leaned closer to her master, staring over Rus's shoulder at the long stretch of flattened ground between them and the cave entrance. She felt her heart pounding, not faster but louder with each booming beat.

How had things gotten worse? Now, instead of backing up an armed attack on a dragon, Cayce was charged with sneaking into one's lair—alone—and pilfering its dustbin. She was no warrior and had no experience with thieving. All she had was a pair of lethally toxic baubles that were as likely to kill her as any dragon was.

"It's not danger you face," Rus said quietly. "It is an opportunity."

Cayce nodded to herself, her eyes locked on the tunnel entrance. "And I will seize it, Master Rus. But first . . . could you build another fire, downwind from the cave? And could you put some more of the herbs and things you haven't taught me about in it? I'd like to fan the smoke

into the tunnel before I venture in."

Rus beamed. "I'd be happy to, my apprentice. I assume you'll want a pinch of clovermint to sniff as well?"

"A generous pinch, Master, if you please."

"Done." Rus clapped her lightly on the back. "I approve of this newfound boldness of yours, Tania Cayce. Great poisoners must be bold."

Cayce nodded but said nothing, staring expectantly at her master.

Rus blinked, then bowed with an exaggerated flourish. "Great poisoners must also be alive, I'm told." The stout man straightened up, dipped a hand into the pocket of his waistcoat, and dropped a clump of green clover into Cayce's hand.

Rus tipped his hat. "I'll get started on that fire."

Twenty minutes later, Cayce stepped into the dark recesses of the dragon's cave. She held a cluster of clovermint tight against her nose and lips. A clear gem in the center of her headdress glowed softly, casting enough light for her to see while leaving her hands free for the task at hand.

There was a faint stale breeze flowing out of the tunnel, so the waft from Rus's fire was not penetrating far past the entrance. Cayce waved her empty pack in front of her as she walked to help make sure that anything inside the cave would meet Rus's sleeping agent before it met her.

Not that she needed to go very far to collect the first part of her payload. Rus was correct, there were plenty of old scales here. The floor was littered with them and the outward flow of air had heaped them into piles along the lower lip of the cave entrance. Cayce forced herself to ignore the steady pounding of her pulse and crouched down on one knee. She placed the open pack on the cave floor with one hand while the other kept the clovermint filter over her face. Her eyes grew more and more accustomed to the dank interior as she carefully swept old dragon scales into her pack.

Many of the dried, brittle scales cracked and shattered as she touched them, crumbling to a fine powder that glinted in the low light. They seemed as if they could have been from the vivid blue-white dragon she had seen earlier, but only if they had been sloughed decades ago. There was a palpable sense of age about them, the kind of heady sensation she sometimes got from examining one of Master Rus's most ancient scrolls.

She wondered exactly how old this monster was. It had begun marauding in Hask's and Kula's territories roughly one year ago, but it was clearly a full-grown adult. Why had it suddenly decided to expand its hunting ground? It had been happy to sit in its mountain and torment Vaan's people for decades, according to the pixie's story. It struck Cayce once more how dangerous it was that their client-guide would not or could not tell them everything he knew.

Something stirred deep within the mountain. Cayce felt it in the walls of the cave, in

the gust of fetid air that blew past her, and in the cold terror-sweat that broke out along her spine. She quickly shoveled one more armload of scales into the pack, hoisted it onto her shoulder, went back to the entrance, and crawled out.

The sun had fully risen, and the rocky bowl was blindingly bright to Cayce. Squinting, she held the pack out straight in one hand and took several clumsy steps forward.

Someone grabbed her by the arm and hauled her down. Cayce struggled for a moment under the heavy weight of an unfamiliar body until Rus's voice hissed, "Lie still, girl. I've come to relieve you of your burden."

Cayce's eyes adjusted to the light and she let go of the pack. As her vision cleared she saw Rus on his knees, rummaging through the mass of dried-up scales.

"Not the halest or healthiest specimens I've seen," Rus said. "But perfectly adequate for my needs." He looked up as if noticing Cayce for the first time. "Ready to go back in?"

"Something's in there," Cayce said. "I heard it moving, coming toward the entrance just before I came out."

Rus tilted his hat back. "Well, it's a good thing I gave you the ring and the skull, isn't it? Back to work, my dear. You can't quit with the job half-done."

"Except when you're working for pixies," Cayce muttered.

"A-ha. Very funny and very true. Now . . ." Rus emptied the pack into a collapsible lock box he had retrieved from the gear Cayce had lugged up the mountain. "Go collect some of those oh-so-valuable teeth and claws."

Rus withdrew from the mouth of the cave as Cayce prepared to go back in. She bit down on the clump of clovermint, freeing both hands, and cinched the pack around her waist. She reasoned she would be beyond the sleeping waft's effect within ten or twenty paces of the entrance, but she still wanted to keep the antidote handy. She also wanted both hands empty to find and collect her treasure as quickly as possible.

Cayce slid back into the darkened cave and waited for her eyes to adjust to the dim light from her headdress. She breathed in clovermint through clenched teeth and felt her way past the drowsy scent of camphor until she could see rough outlines of rock formations and stalagmites. Then Cayce crouched and went on, trying to remain as silent and unnoticed as one of the discarded scales.

Fifty paces in she saw the last glimmer of sunlight disappear around a gentle bend to the right. Cayce reached out once more to the damp wall and used it to guide her forward. The darkness was somehow thicker here, heavier and more impenetrable. The light from the gem in her headdress seemed diminished, less bright and squeezed closer in around her.

One hundred paces in took her into a pocket of hot, still air. She no longer needed the clovermint to keep her awake, but it freshened the air she was breathing. Cayce almost swooned in the heat but kept her balance by leaning harder into the damp cave walls.

At one hundred fifty paces, Cayce felt a gust of cool, ozone-scented air. The entire tunnel rumbled around her, and her hand came off the wall as she lurched forward. Her empty pack became tangled on a cone of rock, and as she pulled it free she fell flat on her face with her arms stretched out over her head. The gem-light in her headdress cracked and flickered out, leaving Cayce in almost total darkness.

A low, dry chuckle rolled down the tunnel. It started somewhere ahead of Cayce and echoed past her, bouncing off the walls all the way back to the cave entrance. Cayce listened to that sound escape and envied it.

"Another unexpected guest gains entry to my home." The voice was smooth, cultured, and confident. It seemed a pleasant, conversational tone, though it was so loud in Cayce's ears she was sure she felt blood dribbling from them.

Cayce got her arms beneath her and lifted herself up onto her elbows. She was almost entirely unhurt, but she could not get to her feet. Her legs felt paralyzed, cold and beyond her ability to control.

The voice continued. "Am I so wretched a host? So unfriendly that no one thinks to solicit an invitation before dropping by, for fear of rejection? Are my manners so coarse, so vulgar that visitors feel they have to impose upon my hospitality in secret, rather than risk a formal introduction?"

Where Master Rus used elevated language and affected manners to mislead and disarm his clients, this voice came with an undeniably authentic pedigree. The speaker sounded as if he'd been living among scholars and poets all his life. As if a bit of easy, self-deprecating banter such as this was as natural for him as exhaling.

"Perhaps you did send word of your impending arrival," the voice said, suddenly bright. "Perhaps you weren't being presumptuous. Perhaps you are instead a victim of some courier's indolence. Is that it, my new young friend? Did you send word that you'd be coming, only to precede the herald who would have announced you?"

Cayce willed her legs back to life. They twitched and smarted, but eventually they obeyed. She brought her knees up under her chest and rocked back onto the soles of her feet, still crouched with her palms on the ground. She kept her face turned toward the sound—toward the interior of the mountain—as she prepared to turn and bolt back up the tunnel.

"What is your name, child?" The voice lost its conversational timbre, smoothly becoming the voice of a lord who is not accustomed to waiting for a reply.

"Don't answer." An unfamiliar voice came from directly behind her, but Cayce knew there was no one there. She stretched out her hand and waved it through the empty air, wondering if the dragon was toying with her. Kula said he could influence his victims' minds. Maybe he was trying to confuse her, to spook her into running.

"Little girl." The cultured voice sounded much closer now. "I asked you a question."

Two flashes of blue light temporarily lit up the entire tunnel. Cayce's eyes did not adjust quickly enough for her to see anything in detail, and then she was blind in the dark once more, alone with disembodied voices and the smell of electric sparks.

"I am Tania Cayce," she called loudly. Maybe if she were as polite as her host he would refrain from devouring her.

"No, no!" The second voice's anguish helped Cayce recognize it. Vaan the glum pixie had shaken off Master Rus's sleeping potion and followed her into the mountain. He seemed on the verge of panic now that his plan wasn't being followed.

"Vaan," the elegant voice said. "Is that you among my guests? Have you been plotting against me again?"

This will not go well for the pixie, Cayce thought. But she didn't need him and had already worked out a plan to save herself.

"I am apprenticed to Potionmaster Donner Rus," Cayce called. It wasn't much to work with, but maybe if the dragon focused his rage on Vaan he would be more lenient with her. "He sent me here to request a simple boon. It is a small thing, something you would never miss. May I speak with you?"

"No," the cultured voice lost its lilt and became as sharp as broken glass. "I think you have already told me enough."

Blue light flashed again, and Cayce felt something hard and warm slam into her left shoulder. Childlike arms wrapped tightly around her waist and bore her off her feet. She dimly realized Vaan had tackled her.

The pixie's momentum slammed her against the opposite wall. Cayce twisted as she hit to shunt some of the impact onto Vaan's head, and they both grunted before dropping heavily onto the cave floor.

The mountain shook again, and Cayce heard a gurgling cough. The apprentice's ears popped as a wave of pressure surged up the tunnel. Fast behind the pressure wave came a crackling ball of blue-white energy that charred and scarred the stone walls as it came.

Vaan threw his entire weight onto Cayce's shoulders, forcing her head down behind a stalagmite. She struggled but stopped when she felt the burning heat from the energy ball wash over her. As the parts of her not covered by Vaan's body tingled and burned, she quickly lost interest in casting him off.

She stayed motionless for a few seconds after the ball passed by, then started to gather her strength to wriggle free of the pixie. Vaan tightened his grip, however, and his small arms were like iron bars wrapped around her shoulders.

"Go limp," Vaan said in her ear. "If you don't I can't save you."

Cayce stopped struggling except to raise her clenched fist to display Rus's red gem. "This ring," she said.

"Won't work," Vaan said. "Whatever it's supposed to do, it won't work." Cayce heard a strange buzzing sound as the pixie's wings lifted them both off the floor.

For a delirious second she was nauseated and exhilarated by the sensation of weightlessness. Then Vaan pivoted in midair and shot up the tunnel. His grip was firm and confident, but he was only a small thing, and Cayce's long legs flapped crazily behind them. With nothing to hang onto and no control over their momentum, all she could do was clench her teeth and try to stay calm.

It was no mean feat. All around them the tunnel shook and rained pieces of rock in their path. The dragon's laughter had become a feral roar that somehow seemed to be right behind them but also gaining on them all the time. On several of the sharpest turns, Cayce saw glimpses of the dragon's face, his teeth snapping and his long horns striking sparks from the rock. Though they were going out ten times faster than Cayce had gone in, to her the aerial trip took one hundred times as long.

Impulsively, Cayce drew Rus's crystal skull and dropped it in their wake. If the fall wasn't enough to crack it and release the caustic cloud, the dragon's heavy body would certainly do the trick. As the beast slithered up the tunnel in pursuit, flashing jags of energy licked across the scales on his neck like bright, savage tongues.

Cayce stared hard as Vaan bore her on. She focused below the flashing teeth and sparking horns as they passed over the spot where she had dropped the skull. The head and neck came unerringly forward, and the sparking body followed behind, heedless and unaffected by Rus's purple crystal.

Unaffected? Cayce peered back intently, shoving the distractions of their headlong flight to the back of her mind. The arcane glow around the dragon seemed to flicker, flaring from searing whiteness to a cool, muted blue. With each change in the light's intensity, the monster's face rippled and rolled as if under water.

The forward edge of the dragon's glow overtook them as they came around the final bend. Vaan navigated the long, gentle arc and sped up through the last straightaway that led to the way out. The pixie dipped and rolled wildly, and Cayce realized he was trying to anticipate or avoid the dragon's next blast. She hoped he could do it without dropping her—or sacrificing too much momentum.

Vaan shot up to the ceiling and rolled onto his back. Cayce glanced down between her own feet, hoping to at least see her doom coming to catch her.

"Don't look at him," Vaan yelled.

Cayce looked anyway, sneering. There, across her relatively unobstructed line of sight, she got her first head-on look at the dragon, lit from behind by the ball of blue-white lightning forming in his chest.

"I said don't look at him!"

"Stuff you," Cayce muttered. The sight of the great beast in his entirety was awe-inspiring, even terrifying, but with most of his body concealed by the tunnel and the darkness, it was a far more manageable sight.

Cayce stared through tearing, squinting eyes. Was it fear or a trick of the light that made the great beast seem to flicker between two faces? One was the face she had seen delight in demolishing the farmers on the

bridge: a majestic, alabaster-horned head ringed with exquisite ceramic scales.

The dragon's other face was fleshless and black, corroded down to the bone. This shadow-image was adorned with brittle-edged scales that crumbled like rust as he came, leaving a faint reddish swirl in his wake.

She looked hard at the dragon, trying to gauge if Rus's skull device had harmed the beast after all. If so, the damage was only cosmetic, for the dragon's speed was undiminished.

So little of this made sense to her. Why had he put a geas on Vaan in the first place? What secrets did a lightning-spitting dragon have for a pixie slave to betray?

The dragon coughed and sent another pressure wave surging past them. They were almost at the crack in the mountain when he spat one last missile that filled the entire tunnel. Cayce fought the impulse to close her eyes.

Vaan carried her clear of the jagged opening just as the white-hot ball of energy blew the mountainside apart. Cayce was peppered by sharp rocks and grit but avoided serious injury; Vaan was not as lucky, taking a round rock to the back of his head.

The pixie grunted and sighed softly. His body went limp, his wings stopped beating, and they dropped onto the rocky ground. The poisoner's apprentice felt two of her fingers break and a searing blast of pain rip through her knee when she landed, but she remained conscious.

Cayce hauled herself toward cover with her good hand and her good leg, inching ever farther from the cave entrance. The secret tunnel opening was no longer a secret and no longer an opening. As smoke and dust rose from the pile of boulders and debris that had been the mountainside, Cayce figured it probably wasn't much of a tunnel anymore, either.

Cayce continued to drag herself away. She didn't know where Vaan had landed but she wasn't going to wait for him to ferry her the rest of the way down the mountain. She heard a familiar groan in the distance behind her and to the left, but she paid it no mind and continued crawling away from the mountain.

"Cayce?" Rus sounded dazed but his voice was strong. He rose on unsteady legs one hundred yards from the smoking pile of rubble. His walking stick was gone, and his hat was torn almost in two. A thin slash across his scalp had pasted the stout man's thinning brown hair to the sides of his skull. He was listing as he walked, his reactions slow and clumsy. He stopped for a moment to beat some dust from his cape, and almost fell. Instead, Rus regained his balance and wrapped the edge of his elegant cloak around his clenched fist to keep it from dragging. He called out again, staggering directly in front of the mound of shattered rock.

"Tania Cayce, attend your master!" His voice was loud but unfocused, as if he couldn't control his own volume.

Deep within the pile of boulders and debris, the mountain began to tremble. Flashes of blue light leaped from the crevices between stones.

"Run," Cayce tried to shout, but all that came out was a shallow-lunged wheeze. She coughed into her hand then her eyes widened at the spatter of red smeared across her fingers.

"Where are you, Cayce? Did you get the teeth?"

Cayce coughed again. "Good-bye, Master Rus." Her voice was weak and strained, barely a whisper. She did not relish what came next . . . well, not too much . . . but she watched just the same. If nothing else, she owed Rus this one final observation in hope that it would create opportunity.

Rus lurched around to face the former south face of the mountain. His eyes goggled as he realized where he stood and what the recent explosion must precede. Rus turned and started to run, and even with his injuries, he was only slightly less graceful and quick than he had been on the way in.

Two large boulders separated and rolled down opposite ends of the mound. The dragon's sharp head slowly rose above the rubble, dust and grit glittering as it poured down his scales. The ruined dark visage Cayce had seen in the tunnel was gone. The grand beast's ceramic scales stood on end, and energy crackled between them. He shrugged and pushed up through the pile of rock, freeing his upper limbs and his wings.

The dragon's eyes swiveled left then right as he scanned the sloping field below. Cayce tried to shrink even closer to the large rock she had leaned up against. She needn't have worried; the dragon quickly oriented on Rus as the stout man scaled the ridge.

The dragon's neck shot arrow straight up into the sky, and he spread his wings wide, scattering the top half of the rubble mound. Cayce had seen parts of the beast up close, but now he rose whole and complete as he had been when she first saw him . . . and this time she was well within his grasp.

As was Master Rus. The dragon swam into the air, his flexible body tracing a fluid pattern up and over the master poisoner. He hovered there, gathering his coils into a series of overlapping loops as his wings kicked up a wind that battered Rus to his knees.

Cayce saw her master reach into his own mouth and rip something free. Eyes wide, voice clear, Rus raised his grisly treasure in a clenched fist. Through foam- and blood-flecked lips, Rus shouted words to an incantation Cayce could not understand.

The winds buffeting Rus suddenly changed direction. The master poisoner opened his fist. He smiled when he saw what had become of his tooth: Above his open hand floated a shard of black glass. The pointed sliver's edges gave off an eerie purple glow that cast a garish light on Rus's face.

Rus lowered his hand. The shard remained where it was. He pointed up to the dragon, and the crystal oriented on the hovering beast.

Mild interest kept those great swirling eyes fixed on Rus's ritual, the dragon's expression curious but unconcerned.

Cayce shuddered as she stared. The beast's eyes were hypnotic, fascinating—perhaps this was how he manipulated minds? She tried to tear her gaze away but could not. She could see the dragon's thoughts and emotions taking shape in his eyes, like a chorus assembling before they collectively sang their first note. In those whirling orbs Cayce saw that though cold interest ruled them now, boredom and cruelty were clearly asserting themselves.

Master Rus gestured emphatically. The black crystal shot toward the dragon like an arrow from a bow.

The great beast could have dodged. He had enough muscular control to move the center of his long body one way while moving his head and tail in another, and he could have slid under the attack. If his tail was as fast as his striking jaws, the dragon might have even been able to shatter the crystal or swat it aside without touching any sharp points or edges.

The dragon made no effort to avoid Rus's black shard, however. The toxic dart punched straight through his outermost scales, extinguishing the blue sparks that danced there.

It disappeared under the dragon's armor and into the meaty muscles surrounding his rib cage.

Yellow-white light crackled across the dragon's face, then cascaded down his body like melting snow. A wave of glittering distortion and gemstone facets seemed to envelop the great beast.

In the midst of this patch of eldritch fog, Cayce saw the dragon clearly. He was not covered in exquisite fused glass or ceramic but in rough black metal still smoking from the forge. He did not have small jags of azure lightning dancing between his scales, but flexible ingots of pale, muted yellow dotted the length of his spine like glowing vertebrae. Smoke and sparks vented from his shoulder joints and from where his wings joined his back. He was not the graceful, awe-inspiring predator that attacked the bridge; he was a smoking, soot-encrusted nightmare that dropped flakes of rusty black with each clang of his jagged metallic teeth.

The horror stood rampant and roaring in his glittering cloud of amber light and crystalline sparks, his neck stretched high and his wings spread wide. The dragon was undiminished, proud and utterly defiant in the face of whatever effect Rus's toxic crystal was supposed to produce.

Earlier, Cayce thought she had seen the dragon in all his fury, that she had seen his true face. Only now did she understand his true might, only now did she know what the stunning mystery the great beast's outward appearance was designed to conceal.

Then the monster hitched and shuddered, sending a wave of muscular force rolling along his body from top to bottom. He blinked. The arm closest to the wound left by Rus's attack stiffened and shot out straight, but the dragon calmly regained control of his limb. As he brought the forelimb back to his side, the beast clenched his fist. The glittering nimbus around the dragon faded, and he appeared as he had before: an awesome, beautiful beast clad in polished blue-white scales.

The dragon lowered his arm and flexed his neck muscles so that the scales around his face stood on end. He snorted contemptuously then coughed a tiny bulge through his long throat. Barely opening his jaws, the brute spat a melon-sized sphere of crackling energy that flew straight into the center of Rus's broad torso.

Her master's scream barely sounded over the explosion. Cayce turned her head away from the blinding flash and pressed herself flat against the rugged ground behind her rocky shelter. When the noise and the dust settled, Cayce opened her eyes and looked.

The dragon was overhead, circling the small smoking crater that marked the last stand of Potionmaster Donner Rus. He hissed disparagingly and spread his wings. The wind from each beat sent a fresh cloud of grit against Cayce's face, but it also carried the monster farther away, off into the cloud-thick morning sky.

Cayce slumped back against the ground and exhaled. Her breath was returning. Her broken fingers throbbed, and her knee was swelling painfully, but she had made it. She was alive.

A shadow passed over her eyes, and Cayce opened them. She saw Vaan's melancholy face and a small, blue-tinged hand offering to help her up.

"Come with me," the pixie said.

Cayce took his hand. "What for?"

"You must tell the others what I cannot."

Cayce got to her feet then cast Vaan's hand aside. "I'm not staying on this dungheap any longer than I have to. I'm leaving."

"You cannot just leave. You must tell them what you have seen." He locked eyes with her, almost pleading. "I saved your life."

Cayce scouted the rubble between her and the path to the ridge. "I'll write you a note for them," she said. "Look, I'm grateful you got me out of there in one piece. But I'm really scared, and I don't want to be here. So I'm going."

Vaan's wings buzzed, and he stood directly in front of Cayce. He crossed his arms and said, "You can't just go. You must come with me."

It was somewhat comical, the miniature man trying to physically intimidate her, but Cayce remembered the power in those tiny arms and wings. She considered testing Rus's ring on the pixie, but the fact that it was her ex-master's made it suspect and unreliable.

Instead, Cayce smoothed an imaginary strand of her ghostly white hair under her headdress. Gingerly holding her broken fingers at her side, Cayce ran her good hand along the edge of her headdress, probing the inner seam of the long wrap where she concealed her needles. Each of the three short spikes was tipped with one of Master Rus's more powerful sleeping agents, and Cayce expertly slid one of the needles between her index and middle finger.

Careful to keep her fingers pressed together around the thin metal spike, Cayce raised her palms to Vaan in an apparent effort to calm him down. As she'd hoped, his eyes were drawn to the broken fingers on her free hand and not to the ones pressed tight around the needle.

"There's no need to get agitated," she said. "I was panicking and forgot how important this is to you. Of course I'll come with you. I'll tell them everything I know."

Vaan relaxed. The bluish tint of his skin seemed to shimmer, and his ice-white eyes glittered. "Thank-you, Tania Cayce." Vaan offered her both hands and said, "With your permission I will carry you down to the others."

Cayce nodded. "The quicker, the better." She stepped forward and, as Vaan took flight to circle around her for the best possible grip, Cayce curled her fingers into a fist and lightly punched the needle's sharp tip into the pixie's neck. Cayce smoothly withdrew the thin spike from Vaan's flesh and hopped back to watch him fall.

Small, powerful fingers dug into her shoulder, and an iron hand clamped onto her fist. Vaan was still standing in front of Cayce, but he was also behind her somehow, forcing her fingers open so the needle dropped to the rocky ground. He took hold of her shoulder and spun her around, latching on to her headdress as he sprang into the air. The long, turbanlike garment unraveled as Vaan shot upward, giving Cayce's spin an extra unwanted boost of torque.

The headdress ripped free just as Cayce's legs twisted beneath her. Awkwardly, she fell, and her hair splayed out crazily across her face. Cayce was blinded and choked by an inescapable cascade of white. Worse, her scalp seared and stung in a hundred different places that until recently held the healthy and firmly rooted strands of hair now dangling from the headdress in Vaan's tiny fist.

The pixie's wings buzzed and he was behind Cayce once more, one strong arm around her throat and the other clenched around her waist. He held her motionless until her equilibrium returned and her view was unimpeded.

Before her the Vaan she had stuck, the false Vaan created by pixie glamour, faded from sight.

"Don't try anything else," the true pixie muttered from behind her. "And don't struggle like you did in the cave or I'll drop you. I swear I will. You can still talk if both your legs are broken."

"Wait," she started, but a powerful buzz rose from Vaan's wings. Cayce's stomach dropped as he carried her over the side of the ridge. The ground quickly fell away, and Cayce found herself flying too high and too fast to do anything but cradle her broken fingers, clench her teeth, and endure the ride.

At least she was moving away from the dragon's lair. Once she told the others what she had seen, perhaps they would let her go.

⁂

They returned to find Kula and the soldiers waiting. Vaan explained what he had seen then turned away, unable even to tell Cayce to tell the others the dragon's great secret. It really was a very good geas, she thought.

Though he couldn't actually compel Cayce to talk, Vaan's angry glare effectively conveyed his intentions. He stayed close behind or above her, always within easy reach if she tried to run.

Cayce considered her situation. Lying was an option, but she didn't see how that would help her any more than the truth. Also, Vaan had said something earlier about Kula's ability to distinguish fact from falsehood. Cayce wasn't eager to test Kula's magic without knowing more . . . like exactly what an anchorite was and what one could do.

So, under the forest woman's broad shadow and Captain Hask's empty stare, Cayce told them exactly what she had seen.

"He's a machine," she said. "The dragon we've been hunting is a huge machine of some kind. He spits out sparks and reeks of burning oil. He's a machine."

No one responded at first. The soldiers all stared blankly at Hask. Hask himself tilted his head, lost in thought.

Kula stood angrily with her fists on her hips. "That doesn't make any sense," she said.

"He's a machine," Cayce repeated. "Some sort of robot. A desiccated, rusting robot." She shrugged uncomfortably. "That or a zombie. He shook off two potentially fatal injuries and came back for more as if nothing had happened."

"This is too much." Kula glared, fuming, though Cayce didn't think the anchorite was angry at her. "Is he a robot or a zombie?"

"How should I know?" Cayce held the angry woman's eyes. "He's a zombie-robot. No! He's a robot-zombie!" Cayce shrugged sarcastically. "What do you want from me? I can only tell you what I saw. I can't tell you what it means."

"I'll tell you what I saw," one of the soldiers said. "I saw a real, flesh-and-blood dragon attacking our fortress. And those farmers."

"That's pixie glamour," Cayce said. "Vaan and his people must be responsible for it. That's what they're enslaved for—to make this thing look like a live dragon." Cayce held the soldier's uncertain gaze then turned to face Hask. "I also saw glimpses of it when he chased me up the tunnel. And outside, when he killed my master. He doesn't look like he's in good repair. I think he might be breaking down."

Kula muttered to herself. Then she said aloud. "That would explain why his behavior suddenly became aggressive and unpredictable. A malfunctioning construct . . . but if he's actually a machine, who built him and why? Why does a machine want enslaved pixies to make him look like a real dragon?"

"He's a weapon," one soldier said. "Like the ones the old soldiers describe. A living siege engine like the ones that attacked during the Machine Invasion. The Phyrexians used all sorts of tricks back then, including camouflage and infiltration."

Captain Hask's stern voice cut the other soldiers off just as their voices were rising to contribute.

"Whoever built him and whatever for does not matter to this mission at all," Hask said. "Nothing changes because he's a machine. He still attacked us. He's still raiding your forest, Ma'am. And we still have to destroy him. The fact that we know he's mechanical gives us an advantage—we know what he is, so we know exactly how to kill him."

Kula nodded as she continued to stroke her broad chin. "Something still bothers me. It's as if . . . yes. Captain," she said, animated. "You and your men have experience in this area, don't you? You've been in combat against machines before."

"Yes, Ma'am," Hask said, his voice hollow. "Two years ago we held off an entire battalion of refurbished Yotians for a month. Man to man, artifact warriors are unstoppable, but we found ways to kill them in large numbers." He nodded toward Boom the golem, and several of the soldiers chuckled.

Kula nodded. "As an anchorite I abhor all forms of machinery, especially those that mimic natural life. I know ten ways to render a machine useless just by focusing the forest's power against it." Kula turned to Cayce. "Then there's your master," she said.

"Former. Master Rus is deceased."

"Your former master, then. Could he have successfully used that abominable stuff you bore for him? Used it against a machine dragon?"

Cayce hesitated, remembering Rus's final failed effort to save himself. "Probably. He tried something extraordinary when the dragon came after him, but it didn't work. Also, I think I hit the dragon with a caustic cloud of something, but that didn't really do any harm either."

"Why not?"

"I can't be sure. My guess is Rus didn't know what he was up against, so he wasn't using the right substances or incantations. Most poisons can only kill something that's actually alive to start with, but there are ways to stop a machine creature—as long as you know that's what you're dealing with. You can foul fuel lines, clog gears, or short circuit power supplies." Cayce shrugged again. "The more lifelike something is, the quicker you should be able to find the substance that'll kill it. Just focus on the life function the machinery is mimicking, and stop the machinery the same way you would stop the living organ."

"Charming." Kula sneered. She looked to Vaan, hovering just over Cayce's shoulder. "I should congratulate you again, my friend. You got around your geas and convinced me to help you, but you also managed to trick me into assembling a squad of artifact-destruction specialists."

Vaan could only smile and shrug.

"So," Kula continued. "I say Hask is correct: Nothing has changed, except in our favor. We will confront the beast according to our original plan, but we will be all the more ready for him now that we know his true form."

Hask nodded. "Agreed."

Vaan shoved Cayce forward.

"Hey," she snapped. Her knee was still dicey and her fingers throbbed. Loosed, her long hair was becoming a handicap. She cleared a few locks away from her face, cursing Vaan again for taking her headdress. She paused. The entire group was staring at her expectantly.

Kula raised one heavy eyebrow at Vaan. The pixie shrugged then turned away.

"And this one," Kula said, "will lead us in."

Cayce spun to face the anchorite. "What? Why me? You two are supposed to be the guides."

Kula bent at the waist, thrusting her massive round face into Cayce's. "My guidance is for us to keep you in front of us, little poisoner. You and your master haven't proven to be the most trustworthy members of our expedition. And you have been inside the dragon's tunnel. Vaan can't show us where the dragon came from when the beast pursued you two. You can."

Cayce swallowed her next reply. Even if she could get by Kula physically and verbally, she would never escape. The entire party had her surrounded, and none of them looked the slightest bit interested in letting her walk away.

121

"Besides," Kula said, "Now that he's out and a-hunt, there's absolutely no danger inside his lair. We will be waiting for him when he returns. I plan to have a proper and richly deserved 'welcome home' prepared."

The soldiers laughed. One of them tapped Boom with the handle of his sword and sent a dull, stony thud across the clearing.

Cayce sighed. There was no opportunity here, only cold, hard, infuriating consequences.

"I'll take you," Cayce said. "If we survive, I hope in return you won't hold me accountable for Master Rus's ill-considered actions."

Kula smiled. "If we survive, little girl, I'll personally carry you down the mountain on my shoulders at the head of the victory parade."

Captain Hask grunted. "We will survive— all of us. The beast will not." He reached around and touched the linen-wrapped sword on his back. "I swear it."

Unnerved anew by the officer's strangely intimate reverence for his weapon, Cayce turned away. She was immediately confronted by the sizeable figure of Kula. The anchorite was breaking off a segment of her live-wood hair band with one hand as she reached out for Cayce with the other. The poisoner's apprentice yelped as Kula's massive palm closed over her shoulder.

"Hold still," the anchorite said, "and relax." She held the section of brown, woody vine close to Cayce's head. The braid twitched and slithered from Kula's hand to Cayce's scalp, encircling the girl's forehead like a crown.

When its ends met on the far side of her head, the wood tightened, pulling Cayce's long white hair away from her face and pinning it tightly to her skull.

A tingling sensation spread out from the wooden band. Cayce could feel it sizzling through her skull and down her spine. It radiated out toward her damaged hand and her swollen knee. Her crushed fingers straightened with cracking sounds that were even louder in Cayce's ears than the original breaks. The knee popped violently back into place, and the swelling deflated like a punctured bladder of air.

The pain of Kula's healing magic was also more intense than the original injuries, but when the searing agony faded Cayce found herself with two good legs and ten working digits. She resisted the urge to flex them, as Kula was clearly waiting for her to do so.

"Consider that a gesture of good will," Kula said. The giantess's face darkened. "And a friendly warning: Don't betray us again." Kula raised and lowered her thick eyebrows, and a rich green glow shone behind her eyes. In response, Cayce's new headband contracted painfully around her skull but quickly eased off to leave a dull throbbing ache.

Overwhelmed and almost numb, Cayce shook her head. Kula had made her point: Cayce was now thoroughly obliged to help them reach the dragon. Master Rus had been correct in his dislike of military and religious fanatics. As clients they were like pixies—best avoided.

"If I do this for you," Cayce said. "If I lead you there and you get in position before he comes back . . . will you let me go?"

"That's a big 'if.' And even if, I wouldn't count on it if I were you."

"But it's possible?"

"Anything is possible," Kula said.

Cayce sighed. It wasn't much, but it was the only option she had. "Let's go, then."

With Vaan hovering close behind, Cayce took the lead and began marching up the ridge. Never work with pixies, she thought, or fanatics. Not following his own good advice had cost Rus his life, but Cayce was determined it would not cost her hers as well.

⁕

Vaan stopped her just before she reached the top of the ridge to give the others time to gather behind them. As planned, the dour pixie then soared up and over the ridge to make sure the way was clear.

Huddled on the rock between a soldier and Kula, Cayce felt a rush of confidence that had nothing to do with her fellow party members. She had seen how high the dragon had flown after killing Rus, how fast and how far he went without so much as a glance back for his mountain home. Cayce was sure Vaan would find nothing—right now, this was where the dragon definitely wasn't, and that was always the safest place to be. Whatever was going to happen to her, to them all, wasn't going to happen here.

Indeed, Vaan's "all clear" signal came whistling over the ridge in a matter of moments.

Hask ordered two of his soldiers to stand watch over Cayce, then he, Kula, Boom, and the other soldiers went over the ridge. They were silent as they moved, quickly surging across the rocky ground. Boom fell behind, and one of the soldiers eased up to keep pace, but the others moved straight to the pile of rubble the dragon's exit had created. Cayce watched as they climbed to the smoking crater halfway up.

Kula dived into the crater with her fists clenched straight out in front of her. Hask quickly pushed his soldier clear just as a massive boulder flew out of the pit. Kula whooped triumphantly from the rocky mound's interior. Soon more great stones and more loud whoops flew from the hole as Boom and the other soldier finally rejoined their comrades.

Hask stood and peered down into the hole. Nodding, he turned and signaled the men guarding Cayce. Without hesitation they each took hold of her and hoisted her into the air. Vaan's strong arms hooked under hers, and Cayce was borne up toward the mound, her feet barely skimming the tops of broken stones as she went.

Without pausing at the lip, Vaan carried Cayce through the hole and into the darkened interior of the mound. The dragon's body and Kula's magic-enhanced might had cleared a wide path through the pile of rocks that led straight back to the original tunnel. Marching feet followed Cayce as she soared along, but they fell far behind as Vaan took her back into the intact section of the tunnel.

The pixie brought them up short, furiously beating his wings to hover just shy of Kula. The anchorite blocked most of the path just by standing in it, deep in meditation with her hands folded. She had smeared some sort of luminescent moss on the cave walls, which bathed the entire tunnel in a low, emerald-green light. Tendrils of the moss quickly spread along the tunnel walls, stretching deep into the labyrinthine depths of the mountain itself.

Cayce spoke. "What are—"

Vaan tightened his grip on her, and Kula grunted warningly. Annoyed, Cayce tried to shrug herself free and earned an angry hiss from the pixie.

"He is not here." Kula opened her eyes and grinned. "Or perhaps his unnatural life is so alien that even I cannot sense him. It hardly matters which. We are going in."

The soldiers' feet were very close now. Vaan let Cayce go, and she stepped up to Kula.

"You don't need me any more," she said. "I want you to let me go."

"Not yet. Not until we reach the dragon's nest and you yourself have triggered any traps."

"What? Why? I mean, why me?"

Kula closed her eyes again. "You still have an aura of secrets about you, my dear. You're afraid, as are we all . . . but there's something else in you, too." The huge woman opened her eyes. "You smell like scheming to me."

"Is that how Master Rus smelled before he put you all to sleep? How is it you didn't smell that?"

Kula shrugged, unperturbed. "Your wretched master always smelled of trickery and deceit. It was hard to separate the lies he told us from those he continually told himself."

"Look." Cayce lowered her voice, rasping like a cauldron hag. "I smell like scheming because I am scheming. I'm scheming to get away from here alive. That's all."

Kula laughed, her deep voice musical and rich. "Now that I believe. There's no lying in you when you say that."

"Then why won't you let me go?"

"Because you have secrets." Kula's tone was patient, implacable. "And my life—all our lives—might depend on what those secrets are, if and when they are revealed. It's only right that you help reap their bounty. Ah, here's Captain Hask."

The officer and his squad came over the jagged rocks into the tunnel. The stones almost gave way under Boom's weight but the golem was easily able to keep his balance and take his position among the soldiers.

Kula gestured at Cayce, and the apprentice's headband squeezed her temples.

"After you," the anchorite said. Vaan floated up, his white eyes wide and intense, and he hovered alongside Cayce.

Cayce screwed up her courage and faced the interior of the mountain. The tunnel looked very different with a green glow illuminating it, but the way was clear. There weren't that many branches in the main path, and it was a simple matter to backtrack the dragon's course. They truly did not need her to lead them anymore, and Cayce cursed the anchorite's suspicion. No matter how well-founded it was, it was still going to get Cayce killed.

She also knew she was on the right track when she found the remains of Rus's crystal skull. The caustic agent inside had definitely been released, but it had not affected the dragon. The skull in here and the black crystal outside: That made two of Rus's best efforts utterly wasted and without effect. Was the dragon somehow proof against poisons in general?

The tunnel angled down sharply, and the temperature of the surrounding walls began to rise. The heat had affected Kula's moss, causing much of it to wither and brown. The part that remained still emitted light, but the light had an angry reddish tint.

Though it was still a wide space and roomy enough for all of Hask's troops to march side-by-side, Cayce felt uncomfortably closed in. She pressed on, dimly realizing that it wasn't the feeling of an entire mountain bearing down on her that unnerved her. No, what got to Cayce was the very clear sensation of an enormous open space nearby, a hollow pocket in this otherwise unbroken wedge of solid stone. Was it an instinctual reaction to something that shouldn't be there, she wondered? Or was it a rational reaction to the party's arrival at their foolish destination?

The air grew cooler, and the glowing moss recovered its green-hued vigor. Vaan faltered behind her, hesitating just as Cayce stepped into the wide, open chamber. Thus she was the first to see the dragon's nest, eerily green in the light of Kula's magic.

She had seen treasure troves before, but none on this scale and none as cluttered and disorganized. Huge mounds of coins stamped from gold, watersilver, argentum, and other precious metals were all around the chamber, heaped against the walls or scattered into irregular piles. Precious gems were sprinkled among the coins without regard to color, size, or quality. There were hundreds of pieces of polished armor and thousands of fine weapons, all carelessly cast around a raised rectangular platform at the far end of the room. Expertly carved statues were piled roughly atop one another, each marred by cracks, scorch marks, or broken limbs.

Cayce peered closer and took an involuntary step backward. There was more than one kind of trophy in this hoard. The dragon's chaotic expanse of wealth and treasure was also rich in the bodies of its victims—the nest-trove was salted and seeded with an uncountable number of humanoid bones.

Vaan joined her then, followed by Kula and the soldiers. Cayce did not look back but instead continued to scan the grisly fortune. There were more than people bones here. Some were big enough to belong to ogres, others small, numerous, and twisted enough to represent an entire goblin tribe. Oddest of all, there seemed to be an entire dragon skeleton nestled among the rotting wooden remnants of a merchant's barge. In the dim green light, Cayce could make out a complete monster: spine, ribs, wings, limbs, and tail. The only thing missing was the skull.

"That standard." Captain Hask was staring through red-rimmed eyes. He pointed up at a gleaming white stone statue of a two-headed eagle affixed to a polished birch pole. "That was bestowed upon my garrison by the king himself. Trooper Fost!"

The oldest of the soldiers snapped to attention. "Sir!"

"Retrieve the eagle standard at once."

"Sir!"

But Vaan fluttered in front of Trooper Fost before the soldier could take a single step.

"We should stick to the plan, Captain." Kula stepped smoothly in between Vaan and the officer. "The beast could come back at any moment. We want to be standing by and ready to strike when he returns, not reclaiming stolen property. Wouldn't you agree?"

Hask glowered, but he nodded and ordered the soldier to stand down.

"Sir?" Trooper Fost asked. "Where do you want to position the golem?"

A low, dry chuckle rolled down from the upper reaches of the chamber. The sound was smooth, cultured, and confident.

Cayce's body went cold. Nearby, Vaan's apprehension seemed to physically weigh him down as he nervously descended to the tunnel floor.

"Better decide quick, Captain," Cayce said.

The shadows high above were undiminished by Kula's glowing moss and were as solid and as impenetrable as the mountain. The dragon's voice rolled down, lush, warm, and playful. "Another unexpected guest gains entry to my home."

Kula's eyes grew wide, and her face twisted in raw anticipation. Beside her Hask loosened the sword on his back and began unwrapping the white linen shroud. With a few flicks of his eyes and jerks of his head, he sent the soldiers and Boom hustling across to the closest chamber wall.

The dragon spoke again. "Am I so wretched a host? So unfriendly that no one thinks to solicit an invitation before dropping by, for fear of rejection? Are my manners so coarse, so vulgar that visitors feel they have to impose upon my hospitality in secret, rather than risk a formal introduction?"

Cayce turned to the pixie, but Vaan only offered his customary helpless shrug.

"He's repeating itself," Cayce hissed to Kula. "That's exactly what he said to me when I came in alone."

"So what?" Kula did not take her eyes off the expanse of darkness above them.

"So it must mean something. Maybe something we can use."

"Maybe." The anchorite shrugged and her lids drifted closed. "Maybe not."

"Perhaps you did send word of your impending arrival," the dragon said, his voice precisely as bright and genial as it had been before when he said these words. The sound echoed off the walls of the broad chamber, and it proved impossible to fix on the eloquent beast's location even as he bantered on.

"Perhaps you weren't being presumptuous. Perhaps you are instead a victim of some courier's indolence. Is that it, my new young friend? Did you send word that you'd be coming, only to precede the herald who would have announced you?"

For Cayce, there was no longer any doubt: note for note, these were the exact same words said the exact same way. She was unable to see what this information meant, however, or how she could use it to escape.

The hidden serpent skipped a line, but otherwise kept to his earlier script and said, "Vaan? Is that you among my guests? Have you been plotting against me again?"

Vaan whimpered at the sound of his name on his master's lips. The pixie clapped his clenched fists over his ears and sank to his knees.

"Stop him," he moaned. "Now, damn you, now!"

Kula's wide eyes slammed open. Her hair bulged outward, shattering the wooden braid that restrained it.

"Done," the anchorite said. With a full-throated roar, Kula sprang up into the darkness and vanished from sight.

Something crashed loudly, and the dragon let out a startled half-roar. A flash of blue light flickered, revealing the monster's position: He was clinging to the far side of the chamber ceiling, his long neck twisted around so that he was leering down at them from almost directly overhead. He was polished and perfect again, gleaming blue-white in the dank cavern air.

Kula's leap had carried her within grappling distance of the sinewy coils, and she had wrapped herself around the dragon's throat.

Both arms and both legs were squeezing as hard as they could.

"Ho, vile machine!" she howled. "Unnatural beast! Let loose your lightning now and let's see how you fare when it gets caught in your throat!" She squeezed harder still, compressing the dragon's neck into less than half its normal size. "Fire, you coward, fire!"

Cayce was no anchorite, and she didn't understand forest magic, but she knew a losing strategy when she saw it. Even if Kula could hold back the dragon's blast by kinking his throat like a water hose, what would protect Kula? She was right on the site of the blockage. When this hose ruptured, she would take the brunt of the dragon's white-hot blast full in the face.

Cayce's scalp itched under the wooden braid. Without Kula, what would control the headband that was controlling Cayce? Maybe the anchorite sacrificing herself to kill the dragon wasn't such a bad result for the poisoner's apprentice.

But the dragon didn't summon its fire. Instead, he curled his head back and rolled Kula up in his coils to smother the anchorite just as she choked him. Kula was freakishly strong, but she was dwarfed by the dragon's body—she simply disappeared under a muscular column of blue-white scales.

"Deploy the golem," Hask said. He gestured with his fist and said, "Battering ram, on my mark." Boom came to life, fire and smoke belching from his mouth and eyes. Under Hask and the soldier's direction, the heavy stone man lumbered to the far wall under

Kula and the dragon. Boom planted his feet, pivoted at the waist, and slammed his right fist into the chamber wall.

The wall all but disintegrated under the golem's heavy fist. A long, thin crack raced up the wall, and the entire chamber shook. The crack slid under one of the dragon's taloned feet, and that foot came away from the wall in a cloud of dust and broken rock.

This slight shift in the dragon's weight gave Kula all the opening she needed. Howling afresh, she somehow managed to twist herself away from the ceiling. Without leverage, without comparable weight, Kula pulled herself out of the dragon's coils even as she dragged him from his perch.

Screeching hideously, the beast resisted. He clung to the ceiling with his last few toes until Kula's strength finally overcame him. Then dragon and anchorite both fell from that great height and crashed through the chamber floor. There, unseen, they continued to thrash among a cascade of rare coins, precious jewels, and old, broken bones that poured down on them from above.

More oily dust rose from the treasure and fell from the walls as tremors spread outward from the two titans in their pit. Kula whooped again and a dread, rhythmic pounding began, shaking bits of chamber wall free as Kula and the dragon exchanged blows.

Cayce kept her footing and covered her mouth against the thick cloud of dust. Vaan had been jostled onto his side, and she reached him just as the pixie's wings were helping him right himself.

Cayce grabbed him by the wrist before he could rise out of reach. "Why is he repeating himself?" she shouted. Vaan only shook her loose and flitted off, darting between falling rocks toward the relative safety of the merchant's barge. Cayce took one last look at the unseen pounding in the center of the chamber then dashed after the pixie. The ship's broken beams wouldn't provide perfect protection against a cave-in, but they were better than nothing.

Just as Cayce reached the tangle of shattered planks and broken decking, a powerful shockwave sent her hurtling through the air. Cayce covered her face with her arms as she crashed through the side of the merchant ship. If the bulkhead hadn't been so old and flimsy, Cayce might have been smeared across it. Instead she burst through the rotten wooden wall almost without resistance. She landed on her back and skidded painfully across the cave floor, bruised instead of broken.

Elsewhere in the chamber, Captain Hask brandished his special sword still in its sheath. The other soldiers fell in alongside and behind Boom as the golem trudged toward the center of the battle. Nearby, Vaan hovered over the headless dragon skeleton Cayce had spotted earlier. Beyond the pixie, Kula and the dragon emerged from their hole.

The anchorite had grown to enormous size, standing half as tall as the dragon himself. The huge chamber seemed cramped and crowded with two giants occupying it, Kula wreathed in green light and the dragon shedding showers of white-hot sparks. The forest warrior had her arms wrapped tightly around the beast's neck just behind his head. He was trying to toss her aside but could only manage to lift her off the ground. Free from their duty of holding Kula up, the anchorite's legs slammed into the dragon's torso. Kula kicked with her feet and twisted with her arms in a blur of furious motion, howling and screaming in guttural forest-talk.

Though nearly transfixed by the sight of Kula rampant, Cayce still noticed Vaan hovering and staring down at her. She glanced over at the pixie and saw the anguished longing in his eyes.

"What?" she said, exasperated. "If it's important enough for you to tell me, the spell guarantees you can't." Vaan only smiled helplessly, and flitted a few feet closer to the combatants.

The dragon let out a roar of frustration. He lunged forward with Kula still clamped behind his skull and forced his head and the giantess deep into the solid walls of the chamber. As he drove into the crumbling rock, the dragon raised the scales on his neck so that their razor edges stood out like the quills on a porcupine. Then the beast twisted in Kula's grip, slicing a thousand vicious furrows in her flesh.

Kula cried out in pain but never relaxed her grip. If anything, the mad anchorite clutched even tighter as the bladelike scales dug into her body. She kicked harder, and more furiously, though the sharp points of the dragon's scales punched through the soles and balls of her feet with each blow.

At last, the anchorite's hold faltered. The dragon wrenched himself loose in a spray of ghastly red mist. As he slithered clear of Kula, he swatted the anchorite away with his tail before she could renew her grip. The dragon's tail spikes scored Kula's face, and the forest woman was hurled backward. The anchorite shrank back to her original size as she fell among the tumbling boulders.

Essentially undamaged, the dragon crawled up onto the rectangular platform. He turned and hissed at Kula, ignoring the seemingly minor threat of four soldiers and a stone man who glowed at the seams. As the dragon's angry challenge faded, Captain Hask's voice rolled across the chamber.

"Deploy the golem. Heavy demolition, on my mark."

The soldiers fell back from Boom, who had begun to whine and creak like an overheated kettle. Orange fire flared from the seams around his ankles, elbows, and shoulders. Boom bent stiffly at the waist and knees, and the stone man held this awkward posture for a moment. Then there was an explosion at his feet, and Boom shot into the air on a column of colorful flame.

The golem blasted into the dragon's chest like a man-shaped cannonball. Cayce saw some of the upright scales shatter like glass before orange flame engulfed the golem with a dull, muffled thump. The dragon's eyes widened as the same orange flames erupted from his back. Boom's attack had punched clear through the beast's body and gone on to char the wall beyond.

The dragon staggered back and fell heavily onto his side. He still held his head defiantly aloft on his undamaged neck, but the huge pectoral and stomach muscles that anchored his neck were longer connected.

Twenty feet from Cayce, Boom's empty shell clattered to the ground. The golem's body was intact, but the stone form that had been filled with churning, fiery energy was now an empty, hollow husk.

"Don't touch him!" Trooper Fost shouted from the far side of the cavern. "He's still hot. Stay clear until he gets back on his feet."

Cayce made a half-hearted sign so Fost would see she understood. Looking at the golem, she didn't think Boom would be back on his feet any time soon, but she was happy to obey Fost's injunction to stay away from the walking explosive device.

Over on the rectangular platform, the dragon stirred. His head rose over his holed torso, and somehow the torso rose after it like a fakir-charmed snake. The gaping, smoking hole in his body was beginning to close as tiny sparks of gold shimmered along the edges of the wound. The sparks seemed to be repairing the damage, rebuilding the dragon's organs, bones, skin, and scales from the inside out. As the gold light restored the brute to fighting capacity, a strange bluish light danced across the headless dragon skeleton beside Cayce.

Cayce blinked, her dry eyes popping. The dragon wasn't just a machine, he was a self-repairing machine. And whatever magical method of self-repair he was using, it was somehow tied to the incomplete pile of dragon bones lying forgotten under the wreck of the wooden ship.

Outside the ship, Kula leaped back into the battle. She was again human-sized, but her hair had grown wild and long, extending around her head like a thorn thicket. Her hands glowed with green eldritch light, and she seemed to be doing a complicated dance, carving intricate shapes in the air as she glided toward her foe. Kula shouted something in the language of anchorites then extended her hands toward the dragon. The green glow leaped from her body to the dragon's, enveloping him in verdant light.

Thick reddish rust spread across the dragon. Then this scabby coating faded to a dusty brown. As with Rus's toxic crystal, however, the dragon was merely inconvenienced by this subtle attack. Damn, Cayce thought, he's already leaving crusty flakes of his own all over the chamber. How would another layer of corrosion make any difference?

It was pointless. Neither their carefully planned assault nor their special anti-machine tactics would work until they solved the dragon's ultimate secret. He was impossible to kill if he instantly recovered after each of their attacks.

If Vaan could tell them the answer, they'd be laughing. But how could you get someone to say what they simply could not say?

Thinking quickly, Cayce turned to Vaan and said, "You use glamour to make us see things. Things you pixies want us to see." Cayce dashed in front of the hovering blue man, locking eyes with him. "Show me," she said. "Highlight everything in here that's valuable to the dragon."

He didn't understand at first, but Vaan's eyes widened when he realized what Cayce had just made it possible for him to do. He grinned as tears welled up in his eyes.

"Done," he said.

Vaan concentrated, fixing his otherworldly white eyes on Cayce. She blinked again, and when she opened her eyes she was treated to the exact same scene, only now the treasure trove was a collection of bright, gleaming lights. Every coin, every jewel, every broken bit of statuary was shining silver-white, as if the coins and rubies and polished steel had been replaced with solid energy. Gold, silver, and white brilliance sparkled, scintillated, and gleamed throughout the chamber.

Around Cayce, beams of solid light crisscrossed among piles of coins that sparkled like stars. Lustrous tapestries, statues, and plate-sized discs competed for her eye against fine-cut gemstones that gleamed like the sun on shards of a mirror. The radiance wrinkled Cayce's eyes as it hit her from every angle. Even the old bones and bits of armor glowed and shone as valued symbols of the dragon's victorious past.

As Cayce expected, showing her the dragon's proudest possessions wasn't a violation of Vaan's geas. After all, there was nothing secret or dangerous in knowing dragons valued wealth and conquest. Her heart pounding, Cayce turned to the headless skeleton.

There was no glow around this particular item. In fact, there was a black emptiness among all that shining treasure, a skeleton-shaped hole in the avalanche of dazzling brilliance. Aside from the odd broken stone and the rotting timbers of the merchant ship, everything else in the cave had been tagged by Vaan's magic. To Cayce's eye, everything but the skeleton was clearly marked as valuable, shining with importance as if each reflected the pride it inspired in its owner.

Cayce stopped. "Thank-you."

"You're welc—" Vaan's words were cut off mid-syllable, interrupted by a wet slashing sound and a spray of blue-black liquid.

Smiling helplessly, Vaan cast his white eyes down to his own chest. Cayce followed his gaze to the bladelike tip of the dragon's tail, which now protruded several inches from the pixie's breastbone.

Cayce glanced into the stricken pixie's eyes. Behind him, the tail curled and looped all the way across the chamber to where the dragon was getting the best of Kula. He had her pinned against a massive column of rock with one disdainful, clawed hand. The beast let Kula up then butted her aside with a long thrust of his neck. Eyes glittering, the dragon twisted his face back toward the little blue morsel skewered on the end of his tail.

"Vaan." The dragon leered through narrow eyes, his lips pulled back into a cruel smile. "Is that you among my guests? Have you been plotting against me again?"

Instead of looking to his master, Vaan lunged forward and grabbed Cayce by the shoulders. Fortunately, the pixie's arms were long enough to keep the tip of the dragon's tail from stabbing Cayce as well, especially with her own arms pressing him away.

"Listen," Vaan said. "Listen . . . to me . . . now. . . ."

Across the chamber, the dragon roared. He jerked his tail away, whipping Vaan out of Cayce's arms. With the pixie still flailing on his tail, the brute stood tall, blue sparks churning and glittering across his completely restored chest.

Near the opposite wall, standing on a shelf of broken rock, Captain Hask held his special sword aloft. As he had when Rus launched his last-ditch effort, the dragon paused and watched as Hask prepared to unleash whatever he had held in reserve. Hask was ranting, wild-eyed, and Cayce quickly counted three dead soldiers scattered around the captain's feet. Without Boom or Kula, the soldiers were little more than grist for the mill.

"Behold," the crazed officer shouted. "The Twice-Drawn Sword, the Hand of Righteous Retribution. Blessed by the High Primate of Angelfire and the Serran Mother Superior alike, it will burn you to slag and ashes, unclean thing."

"Captain Hask," Cayce yelled. "Over here!"

"The sword is drawn only in the cause of holy justice," the officer wailed. As he spoke, Hask undid the bindings that kept the sword sealed in its scabbard. "Any who stand before it shall be smitten. It can only be drawn twice."

"Hask! Listen to me!"

But the soldier paid no heed. "First," he bellowed. "In anger, and only anger, as outrage is the true spark that becomes the fire of retribution." Hask slid the scabbard an inch up the foot-wide blade. Piercing white light spilled out and curled to ash the officer's eyebrows and the ends of his sweat-soaked hair.

Recognizing the tone and cadence of a powerful incantation, Cayce slid back behind the timbers of the ship. Hask's trump card was his to play, but she feared the noble captain was as doomed as her ignoble master had been. Battling the dragon head-on was futile; the skeleton was somehow the key.

Hask drew the sword. Light poured from the blessed blade, consuming the captain, the dragon, the hoard, and the cavern. The last thing Cayce saw before the Hand of Righteous Retribution consumed her as well was a small, winged, blue-tinged figure that positioned himself between her and the advancing wave of white.

Cayce awoke on the rounded peak of a grassy hill. The sky was blue and full of clean white clouds. A floral-scented breeze wafted by.

"This is an illusion," Cayce said. "Pixie glamour. Vaan? Are you doing this? Or have I defied Master Rus's predictions after all and gone to paradise?"

A healthy buzzing sound accompanied the pixie as he descended from above. Vaan was no longer dour and drawn, no longer pierced by a dragon tail, but healthy, whole, and relaxed.

"Thank-you, Tania Cayce." Vaan hovered just over the top of the grassy peak.

"What for? I think we're both dead."

"You are neither dead nor dying. And because of you, my perpetual life-in-death can finally end."

"How? What do you mean?"

"You have correctly guessed the dragon's weakness: the skeleton and that abhorrent metal shell must both be destroyed together. In one fell swoop."

"Well, I can't do much about it now," Cayce said. "Hask may have already done it. He probably also destroyed himself, you, and me in the process."

Vaan shook his head. "Hask did extraordinary damage to the impostor's body, but that will never be enough. You must use the Hand of Righteous Retribution to finish this once and for all."

"Me? How? I don't know any of the ritual he was performing to make it work. And didn't he say it could only be drawn twice?"

"Hask is a fool," Vaan said bitterly, "but I needed him to bring the sword—it truly is powerful enough to slay the beast if properly employed. Yes, the Hand of Righteous Retribution has been drawn once, in anger as the ritual demands. Hask believes it can only be drawn once more, in wisdom. For anger is the spark that begins retribution, but wisdom is the only path to true justice."

"I don't have wisdom," Cayce said. "I hardly have anger, to tell you the truth. All I feel right now is fatigue and fear. Plus, I haven't been righteous in a long, long time. Somehow I don't think I'm the one to summon the full power of the sword."

"The Hand is a weapon that anyone can use at any time, provided they allow its enchanted energy to build up between uses. The restrictions Hask follows are merely an ancient ruse perpetuated by priests and generals to prevent the Hand's wielder from running rampant with it."

Cayce paused. "It's a lie?"

"A long-held and well-guarded lie. But I was able to learn the truth behind it . . . as you have done. This counts as wisdom, Tania Cayce, which should put your mind at ease when you take up the sword. Listen to me now: I will give you more wisdom, complete wisdom, and you will set me free."

"I will?" Cayce was growing increasingly uncomfortable. "I don't even know where we are right now."

"We are still in the cave. I have taken you here to tell you the dragon's final secret, the one that will destroy him once and for all."

"So, we're actually lying unconscious in the cave, cooking in the light of Hask's vengeance sword."

"In a manner of speaking. You are in no mortal danger, but time is precious. I must tell you how to defeat the machine beast."

"How can you do that with the geas still in place?"

Vaan smiled helplessly. "Behold: the origin of our misery."

The hilltop shimmered and ran like melting wax. When the scene solidified, Cayce was back in the dragon's treasure trove, only now it was well lit, meticulously ordered, and immaculately maintained.

"My people were enslaved," Vaan's voice said. In the vision, Cayce saw the familiar form of a huge blue-and-white scaled dragon. He sat regally on the chamber platform atop a carefully constructed mound of diamonds and platinum coins. Dozens of tiny pixies danced in the air around the great beast, showering him with reflective dust.

"Zumaki of the Bottomless Pool was not a harsh master," Vaan said. "He was an old dragon, and he had already amassed enough treasure to sustain him and entertain him for the rest of his long life. In his dotage, however, he found a new kind of bauble to delight his eye: pixie glamour."

Silent as a sleepwalker, Cayce watched as a score of tiny blue men and women circled the great dragon, singing a joyful song as they filled the air with illusory magic.

"But glamour and wish fulfillment can be a burden on the strongest of wills," Vaan said. "As the mind is indulged, the body and spirit suffer. Grander, more absorbing fantasies become compelling, even compulsory. The longer you indulge your innermost desires, the harder it is to live in the real world.

"Zumaki was an old dragon, and a powerful one. He had the power to imprint his mind on lesser ones, to force his will upon the weak and undisciplined. So his mind was especially resistant to the corrosive allure of glamour. If the machine dragon hadn't come, Zumaki would have probably lived another hundred years and died of old age before he ever felt the negative effects of our magic."

The scene before Cayce changed. The glowing lights of the treasure trove dimmed as a half-wrecked, smoking horror dragged itself into the chamber.

"It was a fak mawa," Vaan said. "A living engine of destruction in the shape of a dragon. They came by the hundreds during the Machine Invasion, and this one came to us bearing wounds from some titanic battle. During that battle, its opponent had torn it to pieces and seared almost half of its body away. We never knew how long it wandered after sustaining its terrible injuries. Months? Years? Decades? It was never truly alive, but by the time it reached Zumaki's mountain it was more than half-dead."

The pixies fled from the broken, sputtering machine. Zumaki, his expression dull as if he'd just come out of a deep sleep, hissed at the metal horror. Power sparked in his eyes, and Zumaki focused on the machine's half-ruined head.

"I believe now it was some kind of infiltrator," Vaan said. "Designed to get close enough to living things to infect them with its machine virus. Once infected, it could absorb their bodies into its own."

Zumaki's throat swelled, and he spat a jagged ball of energy at the machine dragon. The impact blasted the metal monstrosity across the chamber. Zumaki crawled up the walls of his treasure trove and skittered across the ceiling, closing in to finish his opponent off.

"My master could have survived," Vaan said. "If he had simply burned the fak mawa to cinders from a distance or brought a piece of the mountain down upon it to mash it flat. But Zumaki was an intellectual being, and a curious one. He decided to try his power on the machine beast to see if its mind could resist his."

The vision of Zumaki fixed his eyes on the twisted metal hulk and slowly extended his head down. As he approached, a cloudy stream of blue energy rose between the two dragons, linking the live beast's eyes to the fading machine's. The connection completed itself, and Zumaki drew glittering blue light from the mechanical dragon into himself.

Suddenly Zumaki stiffened. The flow of arcane energy shifted from the ceramic-scaled beauty to the fak mawa. A tendril of black metal with a vein of gold through its center stretched up from the machine dragon's body. It curled above Zumaki's head then plunged down into the top of the live dragon's skull.

The blue energy flowing from the fak mawa was now mirrored by a steady stream of black metal and golden oil surging up into the live dragon's brain. The two great beasts struggled at either end of this dread circuit, each trying to consume the other while resisting his own consumption.

Vaan continued. "Even in defeat, Zumaki triumphed. Though the machine dragon destroyed my master's beautiful mind, Zumaki's power and personality imprinted on the fak mawa. My master's brain became black slag and glistening oil, but his mind endured.

The vision expanded so that Cayce's entire view consisted of the fak mawa and Zumaki of the Bottomless Pool. The machine dragon twitched and sputtered, casting sparks and gobs of golden oil across the treasure trove. Its body began to unravel and molten pieces of black metal flaked off and fell to the floor, dissolving the stones below.

Above the horror of the disintegrating fak mawa, Zumaki sighed and closed his eyes. The great old dragon listed backward, but tethered as he was to the machine, his body could not fall. Cayce heard an awful grinding noise that quickly became unendurable, then the poisoner's apprentice winced as Zumaki's head exploded, leaving a blood-black smear across the cavern ceiling.

"In death, they defeated each other." Vaan recited his tale's end as a dolorous prayer. "In death, they became one, both more and less than each had been. In death, they combined to become something far more terrible.

"But they are still linked. Even in this life-death—perhaps because of it—they are still connected, still vulnerable to each other. Destroy Zumaki's skeleton with the same stroke that destroys the fak mawa's body, and I will be free. My people are all gone. Only I remain. Only I was spared to preserve the hybrid beast's vanity, to preserve the fiction that he is still the master I once served. He will never allow me to leave, for I would take that illusion with me." Vaan's voice grew low and haggard. "Go I must, one way or the other. Anything is preferable to an eternity of servitude to a mindless impostor."

The vision of the long-ago struggle between two dragons began to fade. Cayce called out, "Wait, Vaan. Why didn't you tell anyone this sooner? Why did you save this vision for now, for me?"

Vaan's voice was sad and helpless, the perfect accompaniment to the smile Cayce could hear but not see. "The geas," he said, "prevents my speaking freely while life remains in me."

"So how are you telling me now?"

The vision went completely black, but Vaan's voice lingered. "Life remains," he said, "but barely. As it fades, so does the power of the geas."

Alone in the dark and cold, Cayce finally understood. For the first time she felt a twinge of real sympathy for the sad little pixie.

Cayce awoke. Vaan was dead but still warm on top of her as her mind returned from the vision. The little pixie still carried the broken tip of the dragon's tail in his torso, where it poked painfully into Cayce's sternum. Vaan was badly burned and his head hung at a distressingly peculiar angle, but his face was a study in calm tranquility and blessed, peaceful release.

Gently, she shifted him onto the cavern floor. She felt the folded remains of her apprentice headdress tucked into the waistband of his breeches, and she reflexively pulled it free. Cayce stood and yanked Kula's tight wooden braid from her skull. It came away easily: Kula was either unconscious or dead, but either way she was no longer holding the leash she had placed on Cayce. With practiced hands, Cayce quickly wound her long white hair back under the headdress.

The remains of the dragon they had come to kill sat atop the rectangular platform. He was almost completely unrecognizable, little more than a pile of half-melted bones and ragged razor scales. Beside Cayce, the headless skeleton sat silently, unobtrusive and almost forgotten. It had lost its special blackness when the pixie magic died with Vaan, but the bones still stood out to Cayce.

Back on the platform, the blackened remains stirred as golden bits of light danced across their surface.

Cayce watched as the golden glow rebuilt the machine dragon's glowing yellow eyes. The glassy orbs ignited, casting an awful light across the cavern as the creature's head slowly reformed around them.

Cayce sprang to her feet and ran to where Captain Hask had unsheathed his sword. She had to find the Hand of Righteous Retribution and wield it again. Vaan had said it would work for her as long as it was fully empowered after Hask's first blast. She could end this if she were quick and if she were just a little bit luckier than she had been so far.

A groan caught her attention, and she sprinted toward the sound. She found Captain Hask under a broken segment of column and debris with his face and hands blistered black. The handle of the foot-wide sword was still clenched in his fists. Either through Hask's heroic effort or more probably due to its special enchantments, the scabbard had reappeared and the Hand of Righteous Retribution was once more safely sheathed.

"Deploy the golem," Hask muttered, feverish with delirium.

"Boom is gone," Cayce said. She reached for Hask's hand and tried to pry his fingers open. "But I can finish this for you. Give me the sword."

Hask groaned and tightened his grip. "Can only be drawn twice," he said. "Once in . . . anger."

"Then in wisdom. I know. I have the wisdom, Captain. Let me have the sword."

Behind them a smoking, sparking head rose up on a serpentine tower that was growing longer, stronger, and more complete with each passing second. Garbled and broken, a wretched mockery of Zumaki's smooth, cultured voice rolled out of the still-forming throat.

"Another unexpected guest gains entry to my home," the beast said. "Am I so wretched a host?"

Cayce turned to Hask. "Give me the sword, Captain."

Hask cursed her. "Never. I must . . . must avenge . . ."

The dragon's neck was now complete, and his shoulders were emerging from the pile of formless debris.

"Vaan," he said, his voice fuzzy and distorted. "Is that you among my guests? Have you been plotting against me again?"

Cayce flicked the officer across the nose. The wounded man stirred, grumbled, and fully opened his eyes at last. They focused up on Cayce.

She flicked him again. "The sword, Hask. Give it to me."

"Get away." Hask seemed to recognize her, but that only made him less compliant. "Give the Hand over to the likes of you?" He spat derisively.

"Suit yourself," Cayce said. With a smooth, practiced motion she slipped a needle out of her headdress and sank the tip into Hask's neck. The officer's eyes rolled up in his head, and his body went limp. As his fingers relaxed, Cayce seized the Hand of Righteous Retribution and hauled it free.

The sword was even heavier than it looked. Cayce was barely able to keep her end off of the cavern floor. Moving with it was even more difficult, as its tip dragged across every crack in the floor and snagged on every broken rock.

The dragon extended one newly grown arm off the platform to balance himself as he leaned toward Cayce. Struggling, Cayce tried to circle away from the dragon's reach while continuing on toward the skeleton.

"What is . . ." the machine's voice squawked and screeched pure static. "What is your name, child?"

Cayce threw herself forward, the sword scraping powder from the cavern floor even through its scabbard. She was now only twenty feet from the remains of the merchant ship and the all-important cargo it concealed.

The dragon sent his other, incomplete arm clutching after Cayce. She circled wide again, staying well clear of his metallic grasp. The dragon's entire body hummed and seethed like a swarm of metal bees.

The beast hauled his regenerating bulk off the platform and flopped forward. Cayce spun to the side, hoping to lunge around the monster, but she was too slow with the sword. The dragon stretched his neck forward so that his head blocked Cayce's path, the merchant ship almost completely hidden behind it.

Cayce stared steadily into the half-formed nightmare's lifeless eyes. She planted the tip of the sword in the broken cavern floor and stepped up onto the hilt, balancing like a child on a pogo stick as she brought both feet up under her. Fortunately, she didn't have to balance this way for long.

"Vaan," he said again. "Is that you among my guests? Have you been plotting against me again? What is your name, child?"

"Vaan's gone," she said, holding his eyes. "My name's Tania. And I must thank you, you stupid, broken bastard, for giving me this wonderful opportunity."

Still perched on the sword's hilt with both feet, Cayce leaned back. The Hand of Righteous Retribution toppled, and as it fell Cayce pulled up on the handle as hard as she could while pushing down on the scabbard with her legs. The sword hopped up from the cavern floor as Cayce pulled and pushed. The scabbard's tip popped out of the broken rocks and slid free, and Cayce felt a surge of pressure and heat.

It was easy now—once drawn, the sword became almost weightless. Cayce leaped up, pulling the blade completely free of the sheath and pointing the tip at the mechanical dragon's leering head.

Cayce hung suspended above the cavern floor, frozen in place by the sword's magic. The dragon opened his mouth, blue-white energy sparking deep inside it. The Hand of Righteous Retribution glowed more brightly and Cayce felt pure power surging up the blade, through the handle, and into her arms.

The Hand beamed a plume of purest white light toward the dragon. It slammed into the machine's head, blasting him backward into the rotted remains of the merchant ship. A white veneer of energy surged along the dragon's neck, stretching all the way back to the platform where it completely enveloped the shuddering mass of twisted black metal.

The searing white beam also continued straight on, burning through the hull of the merchant ship as Cayce had intended. It cut a swathe through the rotten wood and scoured a wide smoking hole before it struck the headless skeleton. A second skin of blinding white light covered Zumaki's bones from the ragged neck all the way down to the needle-sharp tip of his spiked tail.

The sword's beam expanded then, spreading horizontally as well as vertically until the entire cavern was lost once more in a flood of blinding light. Cayce felt herself slipping away from her body as the Hand of Righteous Retribution slipped from her fingers. Darkness took her, and she thought, that's all for me. That's all I've got, and it had better be enough.

As she fell she reached for the last needle in her headdress. It wouldn't make a dent in the mechanical beast's hide, but she wanted to go to the next world saying she had done everything she could to delay her arrival.

Cayce awoke several seconds before her eyes could open. She was lurching left to right and back and forth, as if she were sailing in the belly of a storm-tossed boat. This might have made her nauseated if there weren't also something huge and heavy pressing into her stomach.

There was a cool breeze on the back of her neck. Her arms and legs flopped freely below her and she felt her long hair hanging straight down past her face. Cayce realized she was being carried, not on the sea but on dry land. Had someone tossed her over the back of a massive pack animal?

"She's awake." Kula's voice came from under Cayce's left arm. Cayce blinked and opened her eyes. Through the curtain of her own white hair she saw the anchorite's broad arm swinging below her and Kula's thick brown mane blowing carelessly in the breeze.

"Well done, little one," Kula said. "I promised I'd carry you down the mountain if we survived, didn't I?"

Cayce groaned. "You did. You're a woman of your word. Please put me down now before I return your kindness with a spray of sick."

Kula laughed. With distressing ease, she tossed Cayce off her broad shoulders. The anchorite caught her burden in midair then gently lowered Cayce to her feet.

Unsteady on cramping legs, Cayce staggered a bit. She stood breathing deeply as she recovered her balance and her strength. When her head and stomach stopped swimming, Cayce finally looked at the remnants of the hunting party.

Kula stood nearby, as smiling and as steady as ever. Behind the anchorite came Boom and one of Captain Hask's soldiers. The golem was dragging a makeshift sled they had lashed together with long branches and pieces of vine. Hask lay on the sled, unconscious, motionless, and badly burned . . . but alive. Farther down on the sled were three bundles of tightly bound linen in the shape of human beings.

"Fost?" Cayce said to the upright soldier, but the man shook his head.

"Fost didn't make it," he said. "Captain Hask and I are the only survivors."

"And Boom."

"And Boom." The soldier stepped forward to Cayce. "I don't suppose you saw what happened to the big sword, did you? We couldn't find it in the wreckage."

Cayce shook her head. The soldier seemed about to say something else when Kula called out, "Leave her be about that sword, soldier. If not for her, you wouldn't even be alive to ask. And if not for me, you'd still be under a thousand pounds of gold and rock."

The soldier demurred, falling back into formation alongside Boom. Cayce watched him for a moment, then turned and walked alongside Kula.

They went on for several minutes before the anchorite spoke.

"Vaan?" she said.

"Dead," Cayce said. "But he showed me how to beat the dragon. Even with the geas, he found a way to make me see."

"Pixies are crafty folk," Kula said. "You should have seen the extended pantomime he had to go through to convince me to help him."

They walked on. Cayce said, "Do I still get paid for this?"

Kula laughed. She thumped Cayce affectionately on the shoulder, almost knocking the smaller woman off the path.

"There was no way to carry our casualties and the treasure. Not that much survived." Kula pulled from her pack a melted, twisted ingot of fused gold and silver, which she tossed to Cayce. "You've earned every bit, however," she said.

Cayce hesitated then tucked the irregular lump of precious metal into her waistband. "Thanks."

"You should give some serious thought to your future, young lady. Since you no longer have a master poisoner to apprentice with, I thought you might consider coming to live with me in the forest. An anchorite needs to pass on her knowledge to the next generation, after all. It's nature's way."

Cayce walked a few more paces in silence. "No," she said. "No, thank-you. First I'm going to sleep for a month. After that I'm going to be very careful about who I let make decisions for me."

"A sound policy." Kula grinned broadly. "But you did me a great service today. You did us all a great service. If you ever need my assistance, just whisper my name to the nearest tree. I'll be there shortly."

"That's almost comforting," Cayce said.

"Almost?"

"Almost. It's mostly disturbing, the thought of all three hundred pounds of you waiting around for a message from me so you can come running. But thank-you, anchorite. I can think of a lot of places your help would make a big difference."

Kula thumped Cayce again. "Let me know if you get tired," she said. "I could carry a little wisp like you for a year without noticing."

"Again," Cayce said patiently, "thanks. But I'll try to stay on my own two feet from now on."

It was several hours before they reached a real village, during which Boom said nothing, Kula sang softly to herself, and Cayce wondered how much the local pawn brokers would pay for a poisonous ruby ring.

⁂

The shattered floor of Zumaki's treasure trove lay covered in black ash and metal slag. The cavern was silent but for the odd boom of settling rock and the occasional stream of dust and pebbles.

Something stirred in the center of the black field. Thin cracks ran along the surface of the brittle crust as a small humanoid figure broke through. It was featureless, charred beyond recognition, but it stood firm on its tiny legs. Across its edges, a golden glow scintillated and sparked.

The brittle black sea split again, this time near the great rectangular platform. A huge skeletal head rose from the carbonized debris, its yellow eyes gleaming in the darkness.

"Vaan," a horrid croaking voice said. "Is that you among my guests? Have you been plotting against me again?"

A small blue pixie stepped forward out of the golden cloud that had surrounded the first figure to emerge from the black crust. His blue skin was incomplete, revealing the wires, cogs, and gears within his torso. His black eyes flashed then sparked to life, lit from within by intense white-blue light.

"No, my master," Vaan said somberly. "I have been awaiting your pleasure, as always."

As the dragon's features filled out, the creature peered down at his attendant. "What are you saying, Vaan? You make less and less sense as the years go by."

"Yes, my master."

"Now, then. I'm feeling house-bound and restless. How long has it been since I ventured beyond the walls of my mountain?"

The pixie's face was slack and dead, as if the muscles had been numbed with ice and then cut with a surgeon's scalpel.

"A matter of hours, my lord." Bitterness crowded all other emotions from the pixie's tone. "You destroyed an important bridge then were almost destroyed by a band of intruders." Almost, he repeated privately, hatred choking his thoughts.

The dragon cocked his head quizzically. "Your jests are puzzling, as always. I've hardly been out of this chamber for decades. But no matter. Come sunset I will take in the evening air. Survey my kingdom, as it were. I imagine I'll find a town worth baiting or a small army to play with. Attend me until then, and afterward you may return to the bosom of your people."

"Until sunset. Thank you, Master." Vaan turned his head away and swallowed burning tears to the back of his throat. The people of his tribe, all two hundred of them, were stored far below his feet in the deepest recesses of the mountain. Their remains were stacked up like cordwood, mummified by time, as powdery and fragile as a moth's wings. It had taken the machine impostor several months to figure out that Vaan's people couldn't come back after mortal wounds the way the dragon could. By the time the dragon had perfected a solution to this problem, Vaan was the only servant left.

The morose pixie clenched his teeth and shut his eyes tight, hot tears running down his finely formed cheekbones. He had been so close, so very close. What had gone wrong? He had hand-picked agents that were trained in artifact destruction. He had lured the Hand of Righteous Retribution into the impostor's lair, and it had worked as effectively as he had hoped. Why was he still alive, still enslaved?

"It's happening again," he muttered, surprised by the sound of his own voice. Absently, Vaan rubbed the sore area in the center of his chest. He couldn't remember being injured there, but it seemed as if he bore a special wound that was especially slow to heal. The sore spot was numb around the edges but still seethed at its center, as if something had forced itself free from his torso and left this sharp-edged scar behind.

It's happening again.

"Vaan," the voice was smoother, richer, and more musical as the dragon's throat completed itself. "Attend me."

The little blue man concentrated. Magical light swirled from his eyes and encircled the dragon's evolving shape. When the liquid blue brightness completely covered the mechanical horror, the monster shimmered and took on the outward form of a magnificent blue-white dragon with translucent ceramic scales and long alabaster horns.

"Excellent," the abomination said.

Still weeping, Vaan waited for the sun to set. Perhaps this time he would assemble a party that could finish the task he set for it. He had put every last bit of his cleverness, wit, and intellect into making his false master's demise foolproof. He could see no flaw in his plan, but yet it hadn't worked. He would simply have to try again and play closer attention when he led the next hunting party up the mountain.

Until then he could do nothing. Nothing except stand, wait, and watch like the loyal servant he was bound to be.

About the Author

Scott McGough recently moved to farm country and can now compare the urban, suburban, and agrarian lifestyles. Not surprisingly, his first choice hasn't changed since childhood: All things being equal, he'd rather be down the shore.

Scott worked on *The Duelist* magazine before joining the Creative Team for MAGIC: THE GATHERING®. He worked on almost all of the sets in the Urza/Phyrexia saga and has since written eight novels and a handful of short stories for MAGIC: THE GATHERING. All this, and yet he has only ever appeared on one MAGIC™ card. Though he finds this burden bitter and onerous, he will at least admit that that it's a really good picture.

About the Artist

Greg Staples may be best known for his dynamic comic work and for his lucious fantasy art for gaming giants WIZARDS OF THE COAST. Known also for his skill as a painter, he has painted some of the greatest characters created including Batman, Green Lantern and Judge Dredd. He was voted best artist 2005 by the readers of *Inquest Magazine*.

About the Cover Artist

Duane O. Myers was born on September 18th 1970 in Lancaster, PA. At an early age his spare time was spent drawing, when not working on his parents' farm. Throughout his school years he was fascinated by movies and books that focused on Fantasy and Science Fiction. He graduated from Pennsylvania School of Art and Design and immediately started an apprenticeship with Western and Historical painter, Ken Laager, who had an immense impact on his career. With Laager's guidance he learned the art of illustration and started working with New York publishing companies.

Over the past eight years Duane has made the transition from oils to digital media. His illustrations are primarily done for the book jacket and video game industries.

Currently he resides in Lititz, PA, with his wife Dyan and two kids, Devyn and Danin.